Wonderland Revisited and the Games Alice Played There

I hope you enjoy my new adventure for Alice

Keith Sheppard

Wonderland Revisited and the Games Alice Played There

by Keith Sheppard

ILLUSTRATIONS BY
CYNTHIA BROWNELL

evertype
2009

Published by Evertype, Cnoc Sceichín, Leac an Anfa, Cathair na Mart, Co. Mhaigh Eo, Éire. *www.evertype.com.*

First edition 2009.

Editor: Michael Everson

A catalogue record for this book is available from the British Library.

ISBN-10 1-904808-34-4
ISBN-13 978-1-904808-34-3

Typeset in De Vinne Text, Mona Lisa, ENGRAVERS' ROMAN, *Liberty*, and Allatuq by Michael Everson.

Illustrations: Cynthia Brownell. *www.cbrownell.com.*

Cover: Michael Everson.

Printed by LightningSource.

Introduction

*W*hy do some books come equipped with an introduction? Would it be poor etiquette to read a story
without first being formally introduced? One may suppose
that an introduction might provide background information
to enhance the reader's understanding or enjoyment, or it
could explain how the tale came to be written in the first
place. This introduction will attempt both.

The astute reader may be surprised to note that the events
in the second chapter follow the rules of *Contract Bridge*, a
game not invented until the original Alice Liddell was well into
her eighties. For those who like to have a logical explanation
for everything, there are several to choose from. If you prefer
to think of Alice's adventures as a dream, it might be that the
eighty-year-old Alice is dreaming once more of her childhood.
Or perhaps our heroine is a different Alice altogether. Another
possibility is that the game is not Contract Bridge at all, but
something remarkably like it, implying that Alice is endowed
with uncanny powers of foresight. One might, however,
recommend that the reader ignore the anachronism entirely,
and remember that, indeed, this is *a work of fiction*.

Bridge is just one of many games featured in this adventure, and the narrative assumes the reader has at least a passing acquaintance with their basic method of play. It might be useful to provide a brief account of the rules of each game insofar as they are relevant to the story.

Each game of *Bridge* starts with an auction in which the players attempt to predict how many tricks they will make. The player making the most exaggerated claim wins the auction—a bit like many situations in real life. You bid by naming a number of tricks and the suit you intend to use as trumps.

Another card game, *Euchre*, is mentioned in passing in Chapter III. Euchre is unusual in that the Jack of trumps is supremely powerful and ranks above the Queen, King, and Ace.

Croquet, as most people know, is a matter of striking balls through hoops—but just as there is more to cricket than "bowling a ball at three sticks, and defending the same with a fourth", there is more to croquet than meets the eye. If you succeed in sending the ball through the required hoop you take another turn. You also win extra turns by striking other balls. This is called a *roquet*. After a roquet you have an extra turn in which you strike two balls at once. If your ball knocks another through its hoop, this is called *peeling* the ball through the hoop.

Most readers will be familiar with the game of *Draughts* (called *Checkers* in America) but it is well to recall the rules to those readers who have not played in many years. The pieces may only move diagonally. Only half the squares on the board are used, every other square being out of bounds. If you are in a position to take (which you do by jumping over another piece) and decline to do so, you are liable to be punished for this crime by being *huffed*. This means that your opponent is entitled to remove your piece before taking his turn—although contrary to popular belief, he is not obliged to do so.

French Cricket is a children's variation of the game in which the batsman's legs act as the wicket. Use of a standard hard cricket ball is not recommended!

The game of *Fox and Geese* is a very old traditional English game, played on a draughts board. One player operates a single black piece (the fox), while the other operates four white pieces (the geese). It is the aim of the fox to break through the line of steadily advancing geese and find freedom on the other side. The mission of the geese is to pin the fox down (usually against the edge of the board) so that it may not move. To the novice, the fox's task may appear straightforward but the truth is that a skilled player operating the geese is assured of victory.

Mah-jong is an ancient Chinese game played with small tiles decorated with various designs. Like our western playing cards, the tiles are divided into suits, with numbers one to nine in each of three suits: Characters, Bamboos, and Circles. In addition there are tiles representing Winds, Dragons, Flowers, and Seasons. The Dragons come in three colours: red, green, and white. Prior to play the tiles are assembled into a wall. (This is a time-consuming and laborious process not always adequately rewarded by the pleasure of the subsequent play.) In play, the players (known as East, South, West, and North winds, depending upon where they sit) attempt to collect sets of identical tiles (*pungs*) or runs of consecutive tiles (*chows*). If another player discards a tile you need to complete a set, you must shout out the appropriate word to take the discarded tile.

On the subject of *Snakes and Ladders*, little needs to be said. The game consists of advancing along a squared board according to the throw of a die, ascending ladders and descending via the head of a snake to its tail.

There will always be those who insist on reading a book like this with a critical eye, saying things like "Lewis Carroll would not have said it that way." If you are one of those who find entertainment in making such criticism, I can only wish you well. It was hardly my intention to imitate the originals in the same way that an art forger attempts to pass off his own work as that of a famous painter. But as Carroll's style is such an integral part of the essence of Wonderland—Alice simply wouldn't *be* Alice without it—I have of course endeavoured to model my style on his. For me, it has been a joyous homage. For you, well, you will read and decide for yourself.

Why this book? Nothing more but that my own daughter, having read the *Alice's Adventures in Wonderland* and *Through the Looking-Glass and What Alice Found There* several times, vociferously bemoaned the author's failure to produce any further adventures for his heroine.

This complaint struck a chord. I remembered the same feelings of regret from my own childhood. Hoping that *The Hunting of the Snark* would satisfy her until I had finished, I set to work. She was right: it *was* about time Alice was allowed another outing. I trust that Alice's latest excursion will amuse you, as it did my daughter.

To my wife Jenny, my thanks for putting up with the many hours, days, weeks, and months it took me to write this book, and for her encouragement in converting this mere twinkle in my eye into a real publication. To my children, Eve and Paul, my thanks for inspiring me to turn my hand to children's fiction.

Keith Sheppard
Wokingham

Wonderland Revisited and the Games Alice Played There

Sorry, Will, you were wrong.
All the world's a *game*
and all the men and women
merely players.

CONTENTS

CHAPTER I

In Bed Afloat

*T*he more she thought about it, the more convinced Alice became. Her bed had not been moving when she got in to it. She could clearly remember Dinah jumping up to wish her good night. "She really is such a clumsy cat," Alice thought. "I am sure she could never have managed it if my bed had been bobbing about like a cork on a pond. It's not as if it's the sort of thing one could easily be mistaken about. Perhaps if beds stayed still some nights, and bobbed up and down on others, one could be forgiven, once in a while, for forgetting which sort of night it was; but beds don't behave like that."

There were other things wrong too. Alice could hear birds singing and feel a soft warm breeze blowing against her face— as if in a meadow on a summer's day. That's not at all right when you're supposed to be tucked up in bed in the middle of the night.

Alice had often found problems easier to solve if she kept her eyes tight shut, but this was not one of those times. There was nothing else for it. She was going to have to open her eyes and take a look.

"Well, that really is—how extraordinary!" exclaimed Alice. "Not at all what I had expected."

In truth, Alice wasn't quite sure what she *had* expected but, whatever it was, it was not to find an old, and rather bedraggled, mongrel dog seated on the end of her bed. Granted, mongrels are not, of themselves, that remarkable; although to discover one, uninvited, on your bed could be considered a little out of the ordinary—especially if that Dog were wearing grey flannel trousers and a bright red shirt. However, what Alice saw when she opened her eyes was so completely extraordinary that the mere appearance of a fully-dressed Dog seemed almost normal by comparison. More curious by far (so far as Alice was concerned) was the fact that the Dog was holding a pair of oars and with it he was

propelling the bed, very skilfully, along a narrow and tranquil canal between rows of tall trees.

The sun flickered in and out between the trees and the only sounds were those made by the birds, and the gentle trickling noise of the water as the boat glided through it.

"Excuse me," said Alice, slightly startled but nevertheless not forgetting her manners. "Might I ask what you are doing on my bed in the middle of the night?" It seemed self-evident that a Dog intelligent enough to wear clothes and row a boat would be able to talk and answer questions.

The Dog looked at her quizzically. After much deliberation he spoke. "I don't know. Do you think you might?"

"Might what?" replied Alice.

"Might ask. You asked me whether you might—although it's a very strange question if you did, because this isn't a bed nor is it the middle of the night. I don't think I can be doing anything somewhere else at a time that isn't now. Perhaps you should tell me what you are doing in my boat."

Alice could think of no sensible answer. Instead, she asked "Do you know what happened to Dinah? She's my little cat. I do hope she hasn't fallen overboard. She isn't very good at swimming you know."

"Would that be the small black cat with a white patch over the left eye?" asked the Dog.

"Yes, that's her," replied Alice eagerly. "Is she safe?"

"Oh, I expect so," the Dog assured her. "She was trying to cast off when I arrived. I came over and offered to help but when she saw me she ran off."

The Dog's last statement certainly rang true. Friendly as the little kitten was, no one could accuse her of being excessively fond of dogs. As to casting off though, Alice seriously doubted Dinah's ability even to attempt such a thing. She had often been known to tie the most complex of knots in a ball of wool, but she had never, to Alice's knowledge, succeeded in untying anything.

Nevertheless, Alice was reassured that the Dog thought Dinah was safe. She looked around to take in her surroundings. The trees along the bank all looked decidedly odd. Every single one seemed to have grown to the shape of one of the suits in a pack of cards. There were heart-shaped trees, diamond-shaped trees, a few club-shaped trees, and several shaped like spades. The spade-shaped trees looked the most normal of all of them, but even they looked very carefully fashioned.

It was as if some over enthusiastic gardener had wandered through the forest carefully trimming every tree until it looked like one of the four symbols. She was about to ask the Dog whether someone had indeed cut them, or whether they simply grew like that, when the Dog spoke again. "We shall be there in about ten minutes."

"Where are we going?" asked Alice, but the Dog said nothing. A little put out, she continued curtly, "It's extremely rude to ignore people's questions."

"You did it first," replied the Dog, mimicking her tone. "I distinctly recall asking you what you were doing in my boat."

"I am sitting down talking to you," said Alice, a little smugly.

"That's a trick answer, so it doesn't count," said the Dog. "Clearly I meant why are you in my boat?"

"This isn't your boat, it's my bed," replied Alice indignantly. "A few minutes ago I was sleeping quite peacefully when suddenly I found myself here. I should be very grateful if you could return both me and my bed to dry land and help me find my way back to my bedroom."

"We ca'n't land here," said the Dog. "Just wait. We shall be there in half an hour. Besides, this is most definitely a boat. Beds don't float."

The evidence certainly did appear to be in the Dog's favour. In place of Alice's iron headboard there was a wooden bulkhead. What she had thought was her pillow was in fact a lifebelt and she was covered not by sheets but by some old sailcloth. Pushing this aside, she was further surprised to find she was fully dressed.

She turned to the Dog once more but he seemed to have lost interest. He had lifted his oars on board for the moment and was taking a rest from rowing, letting the current pull them gently along. The Dog rummaged about in his pocket, pulled out a large orange, and commenced peeling it. Alice decided to keep quiet, as the Dog had an annoying knack of avoiding her questions.

After a while, the Dog finished peeling his orange and then, rather to Alice's surprise, he tossed it into the water and proceeded to chew the skin thoughtfully.

"You really shouldn't throw your rubbish into the water, you know," Alice scolded.

"I don't see why not," the Dog said defensively. "The fish here are extremely partial to oranges."

"I thought one normally ate the middle part and threw away the skin."

"Merely a matter of preference," said the Dog. "Anyway, fish don't usually eat orange skins."

"Where, precisely, are we going?" asked Alice, changing the subject.

"You'll soon see," responded the Dog. "Just relax and enjoy the scenery. We'll be there in an hour."

"I don't understand," said Alice. "It seems to me we must be getting further away. Every time you tell me how long the journey is going to take, it's longer than the last time."

"Oh bother," said the Dog, suddenly getting irate. "I'm going backwards again. God. God."

"Don't blaspheme," said Alice. "It's wicked."

"I'm not," responded the Dog indignantly. "I said I was going backwards, and I'm a dog. *Dog* backwards is *god*. Just because it's made out of the same letters doesn't mean it's the same word as God with a capital G."

"How can I tell whether it's got a capital G or not?" asked Alice. "You are talking to me, not writing a letter."

Once more, the Dog ignored her. "It only sounds like God because I'm English. If I were a French dog, it would be spelt N–E–I–H–C, but I ca'n't pronounce that because I don't speak French." He paused a moment. "Do you know what a lamina is?" Alice had to admit she did not. "It's a very thin flat sort of thing. That's just what it feels like, being an animal going backwards."

Alice tried to imagine it, but found it impossible. She turned once again to look at the scenery. The trees on this stretch of the river were no longer shaped like card suits but were still just as peculiar. Each was shaped like some sort of animal. There was one which looked just like a duck. Another, shaped like a dog, was strangely reminiscent of her current traveling companion. All sorts of other animals were there—far too many to take them all in. One tree was shaped just like a man and the bough, which looked like the man's arm, was swaying up and down in the gentle breeze. It looked for all the world as if it were waving to the little boat and its occupants as they passed by.

Suddenly her sightseeing was brought to an abrupt halt. The boat collided with the bank with such force that the Dog was flung headlong and landed in a heap on the shore. Alice stepped gingerly out of the boat and walked over to him.

"Are you all right?" she asked.

Yet again, the Dog ignored her question. "We've arrived," he said.

"I thought you said it would be another hour."

The Dog grinned. "I was lying. I lie whenever I speak. I'm even lying now."

"Don't be silly," said Alice rather curtly. "You ca'n't say 'I'm lying'—"

"Why not?" interrupted the Dog. "You just said it."

"I was quoting you. I mean you ca'n't say 'I'm lying' and mean it. If you did, it would mean you were telling the truth, and that would mean you were lying which would mean— Uncle Charles has a silly name for things like that—something like a parrot-ox?"

"Just because I'm telling the truth doesn't mean I'm not lying," said the Dog.

Alice looked puzzled. "That doesn't make sense."

"Yes it does. I'm telling the truth, but I'm lying on the grass."

"Oh you're so sharp you'll cut yourself," said Alice, but the Dog wasn't listening.

"I don't suppose," he said, "you have a bandage about your person. I seem to have cut my paw."

Alice confirmed that she hadn't, whereupon the Dog started to lick its paw noisily. She made several further attempts to continue the conversation but the Dog just ignored her and continued to lick its leg. Finally, the Dog fell asleep in mid-lick and started to snore noisily.

"Oh well," said Alice to herself, "I suppose I had better let sleeping dogs lie," and she smiled at the aptness of the phrase.

She looked around. There was a little path running alongside the canal but it looked very unsafe. In several places the bank had crumbled and the path had long since fallen into the water. The only alternative seemed to be a narrower path leading off into a wood bordering the waterway.

"I don't see any point in remaining here with this slumbering Dog. He wasn't very good company when he was awake, and his snoring is really quite unbearable." So saying, Alice set off into the wood.

"Who could have cut all those trees so carefully?" she wondered, thinking back to the curious shapes she had seen along the bank. "It must have taken an awfully long time. I wonder if they were paid to do it, or whether they were just excessively fond of gardening. I'm sure there is a special word for cutting trees in fancy shapes, if only I could remember what it was."

And so she went on for some time, discussing the trees with herself (for want of any other companion to share her conversation). After a while, though, she was growing a little worried. "This path is twisting and turning so much. To the left, then to the right, then back to the left again. You know, I get the distinct impression it doesn't know where it is going at all."

She tried walking slightly faster, then finally broke into a run. For several minutes she ran as fast as her legs would carry her, but to no avail. There was still no sign of an end to the wood. Finally, exhausted, she sat down on a patch of moss.

"I wish my bed had stayed where it was. Perhaps it isn't very exciting going to sleep in

one's bedroom and then waking up in exactly the same place—
but at least one then knows where to find the dining room for
breakfast. What if I should never find my way out of this
wood? Either I shall starve or I shall have to eat mushrooms.
I'm not exactly sure how to tell the difference between mushrooms and toadstools—so I shall probably eat the wrong sort
and make myself ill."

Overcome by the desperate and distressing nature of her
situation, Alice began to cry quietly to herself. Almost
immediately, her sobs were interrupted by a deep but
sympathetic voice. "Why are you crying, little girl?"

Alice looked up, but could see no one. There wasn't a living
creature in sight. The voice continued "Why are you so sad?"

"Who on earth is that?" Alice asked.

"Not *on* earth, so much as *in* it," answered the voice.

"How very strange," thought Alice. "The voice appears to
be coming from that wizened old oak tree on the other side of
the path."

Alice walked over to the tree and, feeling slightly foolish at
trying to talk to a tree, addressed it. "Is that you, talking?"

"What a ridiculous question," said the voice. "Whoever was
talking would have to answer yes."

Alice re-phrased it. "I mean, are you really a talking tree?"

"Of course," said the Tree. "What's so strange about that?"

"Nothing, I suppose," said Alice. "It's just I've never heard
a tree talk before."

"You obviously weren't around in the old days," said the
Tree, wistfully. "Once upon a time we trees used to talk all
the time—to gossip all day about comings and goings in the
forest. Then it became fashionable to tell your children only to
speak when they were spoken to. After a while, no one would
ever start a conversation at all."

"You started talking to me," said Alice.

"Yes," said the Tree, "but I was an orphan. No one ever told me the rules of etiquette."

Suddenly Alice had a bright idea. "Couldn't you talk to all the other trees, just to get them started in conversations?"

"I've tried that," said the Tree. "They all thought I was so rude for talking out of turn that they wouldn't speak to me."

"That's silly," said Alice.

The Tree agreed. "Anyway," it continued, "enough of my problems. I asked you why you were crying."

"I'm lost," replied Alice.

"Perhaps I can help," said the Tree. "Where are you trying to get to?"

"I don't really know," said Alice.

"Well, that's no good," said the Tree, gruffly. "If you don't know where you are trying to get to, how do you know you haven't arrived?"

"I hadn't thought of that," admitted Alice.

"Really!" snorted the Tree. "A well-educated young lady like you ought to think more," and it recited a little rhyme:

> *"You can lead a horse to water,*
> *But you cannot make him drink.*
> *You can educate your daughter,*
> *But you cannot make her think."*

Alice tried to justify herself. "There's one thing I do know. I don't want to be here."

"Oh." The Tree sounded slightly offended. "I think this is a very nice place. I've lived here all my life."

"I'm sure it's nice enough if you live here," Alice said apologetically. "It's just that I want to get back to somewhere I know—to find people I know."

"My advice to you," said the Tree solemnly, "is to make up your mind where you want to go, and then follow the path until you get there."

"But the path might not go there at all," protested Alice.

"Oh don't you worry," the Tree reassured her. "This path is an old friend of mine. He can be very helpful if you give him the chance, but if you don't know where you are going, how can he know where to take you?"

It seemed to Alice a most peculiar idea—relying on a path to find your way about for you. Still, she was desperate to find her way out of the wood and was prepared to try anything. Thanking the Tree for its advice, and wishing it a good day, she closed her eyes tightly and thought very hard about finding someone she knew. Then she opened them and ran off down the path.

The path suddenly took another of its sharp turns to the left but this time it didn't turn back again to the right. Instead, it led Alice straight out of the wood and she emerged onto a neatly-cut croquet lawn.

CHAPTER II

Croquet
with the Red Queen

Alice was, to say the least, disappointed. The only other person on the croquet lawn was indeed someone she knew, but not at all the sort of person she had had in mind. It was the Red Queen. Alice recalled meeting her in Looking-glass Land but had found her such a thoroughly horrid person that she had not the slightest inclination to renew the acquaintance.

The Red Queen was holding a croquet mallet, which was far too large for her, and was lining up ready to play the red ball. The black was out on the lawn as if it had already been played. This struck Alice as odd, as there were no other players in sight.

So engrossed was the Queen in taking her stroke that Alice decided her own arrival had gone unnoticed. She was just about to return to the path and ask it to take her back to her bedroom when the Queen, who had now played her ball, spun round and shouted at her. "About time too! Yes, you in the blue dress! Your turn with the blue ball."

Alice looked down at her dress. She was convinced it had been white last time she looked. It was most certainly blue now though. She stepped forward and with a polite curtsy took the mallet the Queen was holding out for her.

The politeness was wasted on the Queen, who continued to scowl ferociously. "If she looks so cross when playing a game," thought Alice, "whatever must she look like when she is doing something boring or unpleasant?"

Alice addressed the blue ball and took careful aim at the first hoop. She swung her mallet but, just before she struck the ball, the Queen gave her mallet a sharp push. The blue ball sped across the lawn much faster than Alice had intended.

"That's cheating," said Alice indignantly, but the Queen either did not hear, or chose to ignore her.

"QUICK!" shrieked the Queen. "After it! You mustn't lose sight of it!"

Alice was about to say "You really shouldn't shout so," but the Queen's face looked so angry that Alice decided it best not to argue. Instead, she gave chase.

"This isn't at all right," she gasped. "In my experience, a ball usually slows down when it rolls across a lawn. Eventually one expects it to come to a halt altogether. This blue one doesn't seem to want to do anything of the sort. If anything, I should say it is going faster and faster." In the end, Alice found she was running for all she was worth, for fear of losing it.

Suddenly, CRASH! It seemed to Alice as if the Red Queen had appeared from nowhere. Alice had no chance of stopping or avoiding her. They collided, both falling to the ground.

"Roquet!" shouted the Queen. "Your turn again."

Alice was puzzled. She had dropped her mallet in her efforts to keep up with the blue ball. Even had she still held it, the confusion caused by the collision had allowed the ball to escape—it was not to be seen anywhere.

"Come on!" bellowed the Queen. "RUN!"

Alice was already exhausted. She could not remember ever having come across a place where it was necessary to do so much running about. She had always thought of croquet as a gentle game. Once more she considered arguing but the Queen was getting redder and redder (no mean achievement, thought Alice, for one so thoroughly red in the first place). She looked so fierce and Alice was seriously concerned, if she did not obey, the Queen might burst. She set off again at a brisk run.

When the Queen was out of sight (which didn't seem to take very long at all), Alice slowed down a little. The grass looked so green and soft that she was tempted to stop altogether and have a little sit-down, but she was slightly worried the Queen might catch up with her again. She therefore continued at a steady but comfortable walk.

Shortly, Alice came to a neat little fence covered with climbing roses. There was a small ornamental arch in it, made out of trellis, and the roses wound and twined themselves over the top. Hoping this could be a way to escape from her overly energetic game of croquet, Alice ducked through.

On the other side, Alice found herself in a beautiful ornamental garden. All around, neat little beds contained all manner of plants and flowers, every single one of which was in bloom. She had hardly had time to take it all in when an all-too-familiar voice startled her from behind.

"Well DONE!" shouted the Queen ("How had she got here so quickly?" wondered Alice). "That's the first hoop. You have another shot."

Alice looked back to the little arch. Apart from being the right shape, it was difficult to imagine anything less like a croquet hoop—it was far too big for one thing.

"Your turn again. RUN!" howled the Queen.

By now, Alice was much too tired. She took a couple of steps towards a little wooden bench, near where the Queen stood, and sat down.

"Ha!" jeered the Queen. "You missed me, and such a simple shot too. Yellow to play."

Almost immediately, Alice became aware of a terrible rumbling noise, and the ground began to shake. She turned in time to see an enormous yellow ball trundling along beside the fence, straight towards the Red Queen. Alice drew breath to shout "Look out!" but was too late. The yellow ball mowed the Queen down and came to a halt.

The Queen staggered to her feet rather shakily. She had mud all down her front and her crown had fallen over her left ear. She looked so comical that Alice had to try very hard to suppress a laugh.

The Queen spat out a mouthful of grass and wiped her mouth on her sleeve. "Roquet," she said, but not nearly so loudly as before.

Then the yellow ball and the Red Queen set off together, although the manner of the Queen's departure was a little out of the ordinary. She didn't set off at a run but went rolling along head over heels. In fact, once she had gathered speed it was by no means still apparent she had either head or heels at all. She looked for all the world like a giant red ball. To Alice's immense relief she was soon lost to sight. "Good riddance," she thought.

Alice turned again to take in her surroundings. On the far side of the garden was a small cottage. A figure in a white coat was busily tending one of the flowerbeds next to the cottage wall. When she had got her breath back, Alice strolled over to see who it was.

He was so engrossed in his work that he didn't hear Alice approach. She cleared her throat quietly to catch his attention but when he still didn't hear, Alice cleared her throat again, more loudly. This startled the gentleman so much that he fell forwards into a patch of marigolds. He clambered to his feet and stepped gingerly back onto the grass, dusting the mud from his white coat.

"Really," he said, "you shouldn't creep up on people."

"I did try to let you know I was coming," protested Alice.

"How?" asked the figure. "I don't recall receiving a letter or a post card."

"I coughed to let you know I was here."

"A cough doesn't sound like a very good way of sending a message to me. A telegram would have been better, or even smoke signals. If you ask me," (which Alice didn't) "smoke signals are the superior method. Your message arrives immediately. You see, I am something of an expert in these things."

"Is this your cottage?" asked Alice.

"Indeed it is," responded the man. Alice was relieved to have changed the subject.

"It is very pretty," she observed, and so it was. The white stone walls were covered in a beautiful pink clematis, which was blooming prolifically, just like all the other flowers. Every window had a little window box filled with pansies and snowdrops.

"How do you manage to get all your flowers to bloom at once?" asked Alice. "I don't know a great deal about these things, but I thought different plants preferred to bloom in different seasons."

"In most people's gardens, maybe," said the man proudly. "But when you are an expert gardener like me, all the flowers bloom all the time. Would you like a cup of tea?" he added suddenly. "I'm quite an expert with the teapot."

"You seem to be an expert in everything," said Alice, a little overawed.

"Oh, I am," said the man. "That's what people call me—the Expert. That's why I always wear a white coat."

Alice could not see the logic of his last remark, but since she had no desire to argue, she said nothing. The Expert opened the cottage door and led the way. Alice followed him in.

"Ah," said the Expert, "allow me to introduce my two very good friends, the Wise Old Owl and the Unicorn."

The two guests already in the cottage were a strange pair indeed. Seated at a card table which was covered in green woollen baize were a large and beautiful snowy-white Unicorn, and a rather bedraggled tawny Owl, with large horn-rimmed spectacles. They were playing some strange sort of game, which looked a bit like a cross between miniature croquet and chess. The table was covered in tiny hoops, marbles, and chess pieces.

The Expert asked Alice to make herself at home while he went off to make the tea. The Unicorn and the Owl had scarcely looked up from their game to acknowledge her arrival, so Alice looked around the room. Inside the cottage, every single wall was lined from floor to ceiling with books. Alice looked at a few of the titles on one of the nearest shelves:

"Studies into the intrinsic mass of bi-molecular wheat germ."
"A dissertation on the valency of basic molecules in tea."
"Fowler's equations for the photo-synthesis of porridge."
"Proof of the pudding by reductio ad absurdum."

They all seemed to have something to do with food, but being unable to understand even the titles, Alice did not venture to look inside any of them. The next shelf looked a little more interesting. She pulled down a book of poetry and opened it at random. The verse seemed strangely familiar yet it was just as incomprehensible as the food books:

> *"To win, call twin! Call it all-star.*
> *Hah! Why wound a watch? Ooh-arr!*
> *Upper buff thick louts, oh aye.*
> *Lie, cur, die! Mountain this guy.*
> *Twin called Win. Call lit awl's tar.*
> *Hah! Why wound a watch? Ooh-arr!"*

Before Alice could work out what this meant, the Expert returned with four cups of tea. He placed two on the table between the game players and offered a third to Alice. Replacing the book on the shelf, she took the tea and had a sip. It was the worst cup of tea she had ever tasted: strong and bitter—barely drinkable. "Not such an expert as he thinks he is," thought Alice, but she was much too polite to say so.

Instead, she broached the subject of the Expert's unusual book collection. "What is *reductio ad absurdum*?" she asked, by way of conversation.

"Ah," said the Expert, "I'm glad you asked me that. You see I'm something of an expert in the field of mathematics. *Reductio ad absurdum* is a method of proving things are right by pretending they're not and then showing how silly you are being."

It sounded a most peculiar idea to Alice, but she did not interrupt. The Expert continued. "For example, I can prove I am talking to you because if I were not, it would be silly for you to listen. Or I can prove chairs can walk because if they could not, it would be silly their having legs."

Alice was about to challenge this last example when the Owl screeched loudly. "I'm not playing any more," he said. "The Unicorn keeps roqueting my queen." Then, in a fit of temper, he swept all the pieces (and the two cups of tea) onto the floor with his wing.

The Unicorn sat back and looked offended. "Just because you are losing…" he snorted.

Apparently wishing to avoid the Unicorn's ferocious glare, the Owl turned to face Alice. "Ah," he said, "a fourth for bridge."

"I'm afraid I don't know how to play bridge," Alice protested slightly sheepishly, but they all ignored her. They were far too busy rearranging the chairs. Either no one had heard her, or her inability to play was thought to be a poor excuse for not taking part.

"Come on," shouted the Owl. "You sit here and partner the Expert. I'll play with the Unicorn."

Reluctantly, Alice took her seat at the card table.

CHAPTER III

Bridge to the Anagrams

Alice was more than a little intimidated at the prospect of playing bridge. She had heard it was rather a complicated game and was afraid she might let her partner down.

The Expert smiled and, as if reading her fears, reassured her. "Don't you worry, I am an expert at this game. You ca'n't go wrong with me as your partner."

He picked up a pack of cards and dealt them out. The other three players picked up their hands and studied them, so Alice thought she had better do the same. She was dismayed to find every card completely blank. "Very odd," thought Alice, "what is the point of cards with nothing printed on them?"

The Expert was speaking. "One heart," he declared.

"One spade," said the Wise Old Owl. "Your turn, young lady."

Alice started to panic. Whatever was she supposed to say? She looked down at her cards again. Much to her surprise, they were no longer blank. Two of the cards had beautiful pictures of diamonds on them. Not the sort of diamonds you normally see on cards—more the sort you expect to see on rings or necklaces. The diamonds shone and glittered just as if they were real.

"Oh!" exclaimed Alice in surprise. "Just look at these two diamonds."

"Two diamonds—good bid!" said the Expert.

Suddenly the Unicorn bellowed at the top of his voice "DOUBLE!" Alice looked up from her cards in fright. There was now not one Unicorn sat at the table, but two. They were sitting shoulder to shoulder sharing the same hand of cards.

"He gets so cross playing this game," the Expert explained to Alice. "You see, he's beside himself with anger at your having found such a good bid." Then he added "No bid from me."

"No bid," repeated the Wise Old Owl.

They all turned to Alice and chanted in unison "Two diamonds doubled. Your bid, Veal Chop."

"What do you mean, 'veal chop'?" asked Alice rather crossly. "If that is intended as an insult, I should be grateful if you could be a little more polite."

"We aren't talking to you," said the Expert. "I know people sometimes say the cards speak for themselves, but I don't believe they should."

"What do you mean?" protested Alice. "I'm not a card."

"Oh, isn't she a card," laughed the Owl. He said it in the same way as Alice's father chortled "Oh, what a card," whenever anyone told a joke.

"But I am not," said Alice, trying very hard not to stamp her foot.

"Oh yes you are," said the Unicorns in unison. "You're the queen of diamonds. Will you please be quiet and let the Veal Chop have its turn?"

"What veal chop?" asked Alice.

"Me," responded a gruff voice from behind her.

Alice spun round but could see no one to account for the voice. "Whoever it was must have crept in and out again very quietly," thought Alice. Certainly, she hadn't heard a sound. Mind you, the other bridge players *were* rather noisy.

"Five of diamonds!" shouted the Unicorns, and together they played the card onto the table.

"I'll have the ten from dummy," said the voice from behind Alice. Again, Alice looked round but still there was no one there.

"Very well," said the Expert grumpily, "but kindly remember I'm an expert, not a dummy."

"Hush!" hissed the Owl. "This is a serious game. Jack of diamonds," and he played the card.

"Queen of diamonds!" shouted the mysterious voice from behind Alice, and at that point she felt herself being grabbed by the shoulders and hurled forwards towards the card table.

As she fell towards it, the green baize covering the card table seemed to dissolve before her eyes, turning into a green shaft down which she was now tumbling. It was like a long green corridor, except it was vertical rather than horizontal. In fact, Alice even thought she could see a number of doors leading off from it. Several of the more distant doors looked slightly ajar, and Alice formed a vague impression someone, or something, was peering through some of them, watching her tumble. However, as she drew closer to each, it would be hastily shut before she was near enough to peep through.

As she fell, it dawned on Alice that there was a curious logic connecting the strange assortment of card players. If the mystery voice really was a veal chop, it was somewhat alphabetical—V W X Y. Veal Chop, Double Unicorn, Expert, Wise Old Owl. She wondered whether it was by accident or design. Her thoughts were interrupted when she landed

(rather more softly than one would normally expect following such a long fall) on some bright green grass.

"Hello."

Standing in front of Alice was a young man, dressed like the jack of diamonds on the playing card. The card players and the cottage had vanished altogether.

"Hello," repeated the young man. "My name is Jack. I'm afraid you've beaten me again. I'm not very good at this game. I much prefer euchre—I can beat everyone at that." He paused for a moment, as if wondering what to say next. "Mind you, bridge isn't my *least* favourite game. I think I like bowls least of all. Everyone is always trying to hit the jack in bowls. What's *your* least favourite game?"

"I think croquet is at the moment," replied Alice. "Hereabouts, croquet seems to involve such a lot of running about."

"You shouldn't hit the ball so hard," said the Jack. "What's your name?"

"Alice," said Alice.

"Then I shall call you *Celia*," said the Jack. "I always call people by their anagrams. I know a little girl called Eve, so I call her *evE*."

"That isn't an anagram," protested Alice.

"Oh, yes it is. I swapped over the first and last letters. Didn't you notice it ended with the capital letter?"

Again, Alice wondered how she was supposed to hear capitals when people were talking to her, but decided not to press the point on this occasion. "Isn't it sometimes a bit difficult?" she asked. "I don't suppose *every* name has an anagram."

"Oh they all do," he replied. "It's just some are easier to pronounce than others. What's your second name?"

"Liddell," answered Alice.

"Not a very good name. Too many Ds and Ls—ca'n't make a decent anagram out of that. Have to call you *Ddellli*—like the city in India, but without the H and with two Ds and three Ls."

"You must be very fond of crosswords," suggested Alice, "if you like anagrams so much."

"Not at all. I hardly ever get cross," said the Jack (a bit crossly). "I certainly never utter cross words. That's my motto, never a cross word."

"What's your other name?" asked Alice.

"Horner," answered the Jack, "and before you ask, yes, I was the one who ate that plum pie, but the rest of the story is all lies. I never said 'What a good boy am I.' I said 'I'm not a good boy, am I?' Everyone knows it's not polite to stick one's thumbs into pies."

"Why did you do it then?" asked Alice.

"I couldn't find my knife and fork. I think they must have fallen out of my pocket while I was jumping over that candlestick. Anyway, enough of me. What are *you* doing here?"

"Trying to get home," said Alice. "I don't suppose you can help me."

"I can have a jolly good try," said the Jack. "I'm always prepared to try my hand at anything, though I'm afraid I'm not much good at most things. That's why they call me Jack-of-All-Trades —master of none. Where is your home precisely?"

"Well," said Alice "It's in England for a start. Are we still in England?"

"I think so," answered the Jack, "otherwise we would have to start talking French or something."

"My home is in Oxford," Alice continued.

"Sorry," said the Jack, "I don't think I know which way that is from here. Let's try a different approach. How did you get here? Perhaps you could get home by doing it backwards."

"By boat—or at least that's what the Dog called it. It was all rather confusing," answered Alice. "I'm not really sure how it came about. One minute I was fast asleep in bed, the next my bed was on the river. It seemed somehow to have turned into a boat."

"I see," said the Jack thoughtfully. "That's the trouble with being fast asleep. You end up so far away from where you started. Perhaps you should try to sleep more slowly. Now let's see. You got here by means of sleep. 'Sleep' backwards is 'peels'. Could be something to do with oranges or croquet. No, I ca'n't work it out. Let's go back to my house and have a think about it."

"First, we have to get off this card table," said Alice. "How do we do that?"

"What a peculiar idea," answered the Jack with a little laugh. "We're not really on a card table, you know. That was just a game. No, no. To get to my house, we just go three times round this bush, up the path, and turn left after the church."

It seemed immaterial to Alice how many times they went round the bush. Nevertheless she dutifully followed the Jack round it three times and then on up the path. After a while, they came to a ramshackle country church with ivy growing all over it—so much so that all the windows were covered. "It must get very dark inside," thought Alice.

Turning left past the church, it was only a few minutes before the Jack stopped and announced they had arrived.

It was undoubtedly the most curious house Alice had ever seen. In shape it was a perfect cube and covered with brightly painted pictures of clowns and stars. The flat roof was attached by means of what looked like an enormous hinge, and the whole structure looked strangely familiar. It took Alice several minutes before she realized where she had seen such a thing before. It was just like an oversized replica of the Jack-in-the-box in the nursery back at home. She could almost imagine that, at any moment, the roof would swing up on its hinge and the Jack appear above it on some colossal spring.

By this time, the Jack had opened the door and was beckoning her to come in. She followed him inside.

The Jack's front room was warm and cosy, richly furnished with sofa and armchairs in soft brown leather. Above the hearth, a large old clock in a dark walnut cabinet was ticking solemnly. The heavy velvet curtains hung at the windows cut out all outdoor sounds, and the ticking seemed to accentuate the quiet peacefulness of the room.

There was a cheerful fire burning in the grate and, reclining on the sofa, warming his feet by the fire, was a large grey rabbit. The rabbit rose to his feet as Alice entered. Jack made the formal introductions:

"Celia, meet my pet rabbit—Jack. Jack, this is Celia."

"Actually, my name is Alice," Alice told the rabbit. Then she turned to the Jack. "Isn't it frightfully confusing having a pet whose name is the same as your own?"

"Not at all," said the Jack. "If I say 'Jack', Jack knows I mean him. If Jack says 'Jack', I know he means me."

"What if you have a visitor?" Alice asked. "For instance, if *I* call out 'Jack!', you wo'n't know who I'm talking to at all."

The Jack looked thoughtful for a moment but soon brightened. "Easy! Use anagrams. Instead of Jack Horner, you can call me John Craker—or just John. Jack Rabbit you can call Bart Jabick—or just Bart."

Alice was far from convinced, but decided she could probably get by without using names at all, provided she always looked at the person she was addressing.

When they had all seated themselves in the comfortable chairs, the Jack explained Alice's plight to the rabbit. "So you see," he said by way of summing up, "the young lady is lost. She wants to get out of here and find her way home."

A deep frown covered the rabbit's brow. "Very awkward," he said solemnly, and reached out for a small pipe from a nearby table. Carefully, he lit the pipe before proceeding. "Got here in a bed and now wants to get out again," he said between puffs on the pipe. "I know!" he continued suddenly. "To get out again she's got to do it backwards. *Bed* backwards is *deb*. *Deb* is short for *débutante* and, to come out, every débutante needs a coming-out ball."

The Jack seemed very excited by this suggestion. He jumped up, grabbed the rabbit by the hand, and pulled him to his feet. Together they pirouetted round the room for several minutes chanting "We're going to have a ball! We're going to have a party!"

Alice was beginning to think she would get no further sense out of either of them (if, indeed, she had had any so far!) when, just as suddenly, they stopped their impromptu dance and returned to their seats. The rabbit resumed puffing on his pipe while the Jack produced a sheet of paper and a fine quill pen from his waistcoat pocket.

"If we are to have a coming-out ball, we must write some invitations."

"Yes, invitations," repeated the rabbit.

Then, with the Jack taking notes, they started to compose aloud, taking it in turns to speak the lines. It was as if they were playing a game where they each took turns at calling out a line and the other then had to supply something which rhymed:

"You are cordially invited"
"(Upon pain of being indicted)"
"To come out to our coming-out ball."
"There'll be oysters on the menu,"
"So you'll want to know the venue"
"Which is next Thursday at Oddfellows' Hall."

There was then a pause during which the rabbit puffed even harder on his pipe. The smoke was catching in Alice's throat and she was struggling not to cough. The composition continued:

"So please make new arrangements."
"You must cancel prior engagements,"
"And be there at whatever the cost."
"For our new and dear friend Alice"
"(Who bears no one any malice)"
"Has managed to get herself lost."

By this time, the smoke from the pipe was getting terrible. Alice was no longer able to suppress her coughs and her eyes were watering. Oblivious to her distress, the strange pair continued their recitation:

"You'll be wined and you'll be dined"
"By us, the undersigned,"
"And all that we ask of you is this:"
"Please could each and every guest"
"Do their utmost level best"
"To help this poor little miss."

By now, Alice could no longer see across the room. There was smoke everywhere and the Jack and the rabbit were becoming less distinct by the minute. Unable to stand it a moment longer, Alice left her seat and went in search of the door while there was still a hope of seeing it through the fumes.

Feeling her way along the wall, she eventually found the door. She was just about to open it and make good her escape when—CRASH!—the door flew into splinters as a hand wielding a large axe came crashing through it. The remaining fragments of door were then swept aside as the owner of the hand—a large frog dressed in fireman's uniform, forced his way into the room. Without so much as a word, he heaved Alice over his shoulder and carried her out into the clean, fresh, air. He set her down on the grass a few yards from the house before returning to his fire-fighting duties.

Slightly dazed, Alice sat for a few moments, regaining her breath and composure. Meanwhile she surveyed the frenzied activity round the house.

Smoke was billowing from everywhere, even seeping out through the hinges on the roof. Parked outside was a gleaming red fire-engine manned by an enormous number of similarly dressed frogs. Alice tried to count them but she had to give up. They all looked so alike, dressed in identical uniforms. She kept losing track of which she had counted and which she had not. They were all rushing about, this way and that, giving the distinct impression they hadn't the slightest idea what they should be doing.

To add to the confusion, instead of a helmet, each was wearing a large brass coal-scuttle, using the handle as a chinstrap. The coal-scuttles were all much too large and kept falling over their eyes. Whenever this happened, the wearer never stopped to re-adjust it. He just kept running until he collided with a wall or one of his colleagues.

The only individual not dashing about was a slightly larger frog who, Alice guessed, was their commander. He was leaning against the fire-engine shouting orders, but none of his crew seemed to be taking any notice at all. At that moment, much to Alice's amusement, two of the firemen emerged from the house carrying the rabbit, who was still smoking his pipe. A third fireman removed his coal-scuttle and filled it with water from a tap on the side of the fire-engine. This he proceeded to empty over the rabbit, who stood there spluttering and glaring at the fireman, water dripping from every part of him. "Serves him right for causing such a nuisance," thought Alice. "He does look very put out. Mind you, I suppose he was 'put out', in a way."

The confusion round the house continued without any sign of a let up. The Jack had just been carried out and had been similarly doused and Alice was wondering how she had escaped the same treatment. She decided it might be wise to move on before the firemen remembered their oversight and turned their coal-scuttles on her.

So, turning her back on the mayhem, she strolled further along the path that had led her to the Jack's house.

CHAPTER IV

Draughts and Dishwashing

It was pleasantly warm and sunny as Alice walked along the path. She could not remember if the sun had been out before she had visited the Jack's house, but she was certainly aware of it now.

There was a neat little border of flowers on either side of the track, and dozens of butterflies were flitting from one bloom to another. The butterflies were much larger than the sort with which she was familiar. Some must have been up to a foot in wingspan. Beyond the flowers there were dense brambles as far as the eye could see. It would have been impossible to forge a way through without the risk of severely scratched legs, so Alice contented herself with following the path.

The weather was far too warm to walk very far, so, after a while, Alice was relieved when the brambles finally came to an end. Instead, beyond the flower borders, there was a grassy meadow. Alice found a gap in the flowerbed, walked through it, and sat down on the grass.

The meadow was almost perfectly square and bordered on three sides by more brambles. At each of the far corners there was a stile, and Alice could just make out that these led to further areas of grass, joined diagonally to the one in which she was sitting.

Having regained sufficient energy to press on, she set off in the direction of one of these stiles. Although the sun was still out, there was a light breeze, making Alice wish she had a cardigan.

As she walked, the wind seemed to be getting stronger by the minute. By the time she reached the corner of the field, it was decidedly draughty. The brambles formed a natural wind-break and channelled all the force of the breeze into the corner.

Looking over the stile, Alice saw the next field was bordered on all four sides by the brambles, but had further stiles in each corner. It was as if the entire area were filled with an alternating patchwork of grass fields and brambles. She was just about to climb the stile to explore further, when she became aware of another noise apart from the wind. It was similar to the noise of the wind—so much so that at first she had not recognized it as being a separate sound. It was a sort of swishing swirling sound and it got louder and louder.

"I do hope that isn't a whirlwind or a hurricane," thought Alice, a little anxiously. "There's a sort of deep rumbling hum to it as well. I've never heard a wind sound like *that* before. Whatever can it be? It's just as if an enormous humming top were slowly coming this way."

For a moment, Alice wondered whether it might be wise to run, but she had done enough running in the last few hours to last her all week. Besides, she was more than a little curious to discover what the strange noise might be. But it occurred to her that there was also no way of telling which would be the best direction in which to run.

"One would feel very foolish," thought Alice, "if one tried to run away from something only to find oneself running towards it!"

By now, the hum was deafening. It seemed to come from beyond the far corner of the next field, and she peered in that direction, trying to make out the cause. It was at that moment it appeared. From the other side of the far brambles rose a gigantic black disc. It must have been nearly as big as the field, and two or three feet thick. It moved majestically through the air, spinning and making the terrible humming noise as it went.

It was slowly moving towards her and Alice wondered whether she should run in case it came right over and crashed on her head. As she watched, though, she realized the disc was already sinking. Having come to within a few yards it advanced no further but sank down, finally coming to rest in the adjoining field. As it did so, the swishing noise stopped. The hum gradually became quieter again and eventually died away completely.

"Well, it doesn't look as if I shall be able to go this way now," thought Alice. "That strange disc has completely filled the field. There's no room to squeeze between it and the brambles round the edge—not without getting scratched, that is."

The disc didn't look or sound as if it intended to move again (much to Alice's relief). Nevertheless, she decided it might be better to go another way. She had no idea what the enormous disc might be. For all she knew, it could be dangerous.

Alice climbed down from the stile and walked along the edge of the field to the other stile in the adjacent corner. There was another field beyond this stile, that was, fortunately, empty. She climbed nimbly over into the new field, determined to keep going until she could find her way out of this patchwork of meadows and brambles.

"Ha!" said a voice, so suddenly that it made Alice jump. The new field was not as empty as she had at first thought. Her heart sank to find herself confronted, yet again, by the Red Queen, who must have been hiding behind the bushes.

"You didn't take me. That means I can huff you," announced the Queen.

Now there were many things the giant disc could have been but it had never occurred to Alice it might be an enormous draughtsman. Even had she realized what it was, Alice seriously doubted her ability to jump over it in order to take it.

The Queen opened her mouth wide and began to draw in her breath. For what seemed like an age, she stood there, sucking in air, and turning redder than ever. Her chest swelled and swelled. "This time she really is overdoing it," thought Alice. "I'm sure she is going to burst any moment."

But just when it seemed she could expand no more, the Queen started to blow. Through pursed lips, she blew harder and harder. Alice was never sure whether it was the force of the Queen's blowing or whether the wind got stronger at that moment. Either way, she found herself being pushed backwards by the force of the air. She staggered back a few steps but then lost her foothold. She was lifted off the ground and found herself sailing backwards through the air. Faster and faster she went. The fields below flashed past at increasing speed until the ground beneath became just a blur.

Then, without any warning, the wind stopped. As Alice fell, she closed her eyes in anticipation of a nasty crash landing, but it never came. Instead, she landed on something soft and springy. Alice opened her eyes to see what had saved her.

"I do believe it's a parasol," she remarked. "It's lucky it should happen to be beneath the very place where I fell from the sky. Another few feet and I could have been badly injured."

As she spoke, Alice slid down the edge of the gaily-coloured parasol and landed unhurt (but in a rather undignified manner) on the ground.

The parasol was planted in the centre of a small outdoor table, surrounded by four white metal chairs. Several similar tables were dotted here and there, occupying a section of pavement outside a little café.

Dusting herself off, she sat down on one of the chairs to recover her composure. No sooner had she done so than the café door flew open and out waddled a rather plump Sea Lion. The Sea Lion was wearing a waiter's starched white bib and bow-tie. Balanced on the tip of his nose was a tray full of empty glasses.

The Sea Lion waddled over to Alice. "What can I fetch you, Miss?" he barked. "Draught beer perhaps?"

"No thank you," replied Alice. "I think I've had quite enough of draughts for the time being."

"Maybe a lemonade would be more to your liking?" asked the Sea Lion.

"Yes," agreed Alice. "A lemonade would be very nice. Thank you."

The Sea Lion waddled off inside again. Alice couldn't help admiring him. How clever he was to have conducted the entire conversation with a tray of glasses balanced on his nose! "But what if he were to sneeze?" Alice wondered. "Really, it could cause a dreadful mess."

Very shortly, the Sea Lion returned with the tray still on his nose. This time it held just a single glass, containing Alice's lemonade. The Sea Lion bowed his head low and Alice took the glass and had a long sip. It was deliciously cool. She had not realized it before, but all this flying around on such a warm day had left her rather hot. She sipped again, savouring the coldness and the bubbles up her nose.

The Sea Lion coughed politely to attract Alice's attention. "That will be three pounds, please," he barked.

Alice nearly dropped her glass in astonishment. "Isn't that rather a lot just for one glass of lemonade?" she gasped.

"It is the best lemonade you can buy," replied the Sea Lion.

"I am sure it is," continued Alice. "Even so, I think the price is a little unreasonable. Why, I don't suppose it costs so much for a whole bottle in the shops."

"Ah, but then you wouldn't get such a fine glass to drink it from," said the Sea Lion.

Alice still felt the price was very dear, even if it included the loan of the glass, but she declined to say anything for fear of repeating herself. Instead, she looked into her purse. "I'm afraid I only have tuppence," she said apologetically. "That will just have to do. Really, I haven't any more. I don't suppose even my money-box at home has much more than four shillings in it and, even if it did, I don't know how to get home to give it to you. You can have the rest of the lemonade back if you like. I've only drunk a little."

Clearly, the Sea Lion had warmed a little at her plight, because he continued in a kinder tone. "No, you finish your drink. But if that is all the money you have, I'm afraid you will have to help with the washing up."

Alice agreed. It seemed a reasonable solution. She often helped with the washing up at home and actually rather enjoyed it. Besides, there were no other customers to be seen, so Alice guessed there couldn't be many dishes to wash.

Alas! She could not have been more wrong. After she had finished her drink, the Sea Lion ushered her through the front door of the café and into a dingy back room. There, beside a tiny sink, was a drainer covered with more dirty dishes than Alice had seen in her entire life. There were hundreds upon hundreds of them. There was a rather precarious pile of plates nearly reaching to the ceiling, a pile of soup dishes almost as high, further piles of pots and pans, and rows upon rows of cups, each stuffed with dirty crockery. No one could have done any washing up for weeks.

"I didn't expect there would be quite so many dishes to wash," she said plaintively. "Surely I don't have to do them all, just for one glass of lemonade."

The Sea Lion was leaning against a sideboard, tossing fish into the air with his flipper and catching them in his mouth. "We shall see," he said between swallows. "It all depends how well you wash them. Remember it was a very expensive glass of lemonade. Would you care for a fish?"

They were raw and did not look at all appetizing. "I'm not very keen on the taste of fish," she replied.

"I wasn't asking you to taste one," replied the Sea Lion. "I asked if you'd care for one—you know, feed it, take it for walks, and so on."

"I'm not sure I'd know how," replied Alice, wondering how one might go about taking a fish for a walk. She decided it was best to change the subject. "You said it depends how well I wash the dishes. Does that mean if I wash them well I can stop after just a few?" she asked hopefully.

"Of course not," replied the Sea Lion. "If you wash the dishes well, you must do the lot. Wash them badly, and I would rather you stopped."

The Sea Lion's remark made a strange sort of sense but it did rather seem that all Alice had to do was to make a mess of the job in order to get out of it. She turned on the tap.

"This water is cold," she protested.

"You haven't run it long enough," said the Sea Lion. "The water here is exceptionally fit. You have to run it for ages before it gets hot. Why, sometimes I run my water for five miles across country and it's scarcely out of breath."

Alice waited a while, but the water didn't seem to be getting any hotter. Moreover, she couldn't find any soap. Without much enthusiasm she dipped the first plate into the cold water. Although she didn't want to make too good a job of it (for fear of being there all night), she had a certain pride in her work and would have much preferred it if she could have got at least some of the dirt off. The plate had fish skin and a few bones stuck on it and the cold, soapless, water had practically no effect on them.

She lifted the plate from the water. It didn't look any cleaner than when she had started. "I'm sorry," she said. "I'm afraid this water just doesn't seem to be working at all." But the Sea Lion wasn't listening.

"Shush!" he said sharply. "Do you hear that?"

"What?" asked Alice. She could hear nothing.

"It's the school bell. Time to go to school."

Alice listened again. This time she could just about make out a soft ringing noise in the background.

"Come on," said the Sea Lion sternly. "Leave those dishes until later. It's time to go to school."

Alice was only too pleased to leave the dishes. This was the worst dish wash she had ever attempted. Perhaps, with a bit of luck, the Sea Lion would have forgotten all about it by the time school was over—or she might be able to slip away somehow. With some relief, she allowed the Sea Lion to take her by the arm, lead her out of the café, and off up the street.

CHAPTER V

Classroom and
Cricket Pitch

*T*he school to which the Sea Lion led Alice was a tall red brick building with an imposing bell tower. The bell was ringing loudly, making such a noise that Alice was glad to get inside. The Sea Lion made his way into one of the classrooms and sat down at a desk.

"You sit there," he said, pointing at an empty desk to his right.

Alice sat down and surveyed the room.

The class was composed entirely of sea birds and creatures. At the desk to Alice's right was a young Pelican, taking copious notes in a small exercise book using an enormous quill pen. He paused at intervals to dip the nib into his huge beak, to recharge it with ink. It struck Alice as rather a dangerous place to keep one's ink. Should he slip over he could easily swallow it, and the consequences of a cough or sneeze would be too horrific to think about.

Beyond the Pelican, a small group of baby seals were playing a game that involved batting pieces of chalk at one another with their tail flippers. As Alice watched, one piece missed its target and landed in the Pelican's beak. Some ink splashed out and started to run down his chin, but he was so engrossed in his work that he failed to notice.

By the wall behind the seals, a crab and a lobster were engaged in arm wrestling, or rather, claw wrestling. With their enormous pincers locked together, they were struggling backwards and forwards, each trying to turn the other on its back.

On the other side of the room, in front of the Sea Lion, a rather bossy looking Seagull was standing on his desk

screeching out orders to everyone in the room. He had an uncanny knack of turning the last word of every order into an ear splitting SQUAWK sound. "Stop playing with the CHALK"—"You're not allowed to TALK," but nobody was paying him the slightest attention.

At that moment, the door opened and the teacher appeared. A hush fell upon the room, and the sea creatures scuttled back to their desks—all except for the Seagull. He had his back to the door and continued to screech out a couple more orders before he became suspicious of the sudden hush. When he turned and saw the teacher, he turned bright pink with embarrassment.

"If he turns any pinker," thought Alice, "I do believe he might turn into a flamingo."

Indeed, Alice even thought the Seagull's legs might be getting a bit longer but then he recovered. The pink faded to a rather more seagull-like colour as he fell silent and sat down at his desk.

The teacher was a rather stern-looking ageing Penguin, with a monocle, and dressed in traditional teacher's gown and mortarboard. He strode to the front of the class and stood glaring round the room, as if daring anyone to so much as move.

When it was clear that everyone was paying attention, the Penguin pulled a small textbook from under his wing and opened it. "To-day," he began, "we shall start with geography."

There was a sudden burst of activity, as the pupils opened their desks and took out what Alice assumed were geography textbooks. Alice opened her desk too, but it was empty. There was then a terrible racket as the pupils all slammed their desks shut again. Alice was sure they could have managed to do this more quietly had they tried. She was surprised that the Penguin did not tell them off. She quietly closed her desk and sat back, hoping no one would tell her off for not having a textbook.

The Penguin had seated himself on a tall stool at the front of the class. When the noise of slamming desks eventually subsided, he cleared his throat and continued. "You will recall last week we discussed Germany, famous for beer, sausages, and measles. This week we shall be discussing France. Now, what is the capital of France?"

Alice put her hand up. That was easy. "Paris, sir," she said.

"Pardon?" said the Penguin, staring at her with a puzzled expression on his face.

"Paris, sir," repeated Alice. "Paris is the capital of France."

"What nonsense girl," said the Penguin crossly. "Now if you don't know the answer, don't interrupt."

Alice was sure Paris really *was* the capital, but the Penguin continued before she had a chance to protest. "The capital of France is *F*. Surely that should be obvious to anyone with even half an ounce of sense. Let's try another. What is the population of France?" He looked round from pupil to pupil, but no one volunteered an answer. After his reaction to her last suggestion, Alice would have been too scared to say anything even if she did know the answer (which she didn't).

"Tut, tut," muttered the teacher disapprovingly. "You really are the dimmest class I have ever had to deal with. Why, the population of France is *French* of course, every single one of them. Now, France is famous for a number of things—French polish, plaster of Paris, and cricket..."

He stopped. Alice had her hand up again. She was getting a little confused. "Please sir," she said, "I thought it was we English who were famous for cricket."

"Of a sort, maybe, of a sort," replied the Penguin irritably. "But surely you have heard of French cricket? Really, this is hopeless. Perhaps you would be better at arithmetic. Take out your arithmetic exercise books all of you."

Again, the clamour of hurriedly-opened and noisily-shut desks filled the room. Although hers was empty, Alice decided to open it again just to make it look as if she were doing what she was told. To her surprise, inside her desk she found a slim volume entitled *First Year Geography Primer*. She was convinced it had not been there when she last looked, but it was too late now—the geography lesson was over. There was certainly no exercise book so Alice shut the desk again.

"Right then," continued the Penguin, "what is the next number in the sequence 1, 2, 3, 4, 5?" and he wrote it up on the blackboard:

$$1 \quad 2 \quad 3 \quad 4 \quad 5 \quad ?$$

Alice was sure she could not go wrong this time. She put up her hand.

"Yes?" said the Penguin.

"Surely it is obvious," answered Alice, "the answer must be six."

"Never believe the obvious without question," replied the Penguin. "The answer is not six, it is thirty-six. Each number in the sequence is calculated as follows..." and he wrote on the board again. Alice could only vaguely remember what he wrote, but Uncle Charles, who knew a little of mathematics, helped her to piece it together later:

$$\frac{n^5 - 15n^4 + 85n^3 - 225n^2 + 278n - 120}{4}$$

"Let's try this one," said the Penguin with a sigh. "If it takes three men four days to dig five holes, how long would it take one man to build a wall?"

Alice was now more confused than ever. The question didn't seem to make sense at all. "Excuse me sir," she said, putting her hand up yet again, "but I don't see how the time it takes the men to dig holes has anything to do with the time it takes them to build walls."

"Of course it has, of course it has," snapped the Penguin impatiently. "If they were lazy men, it would take them a long time to dig holes; if they were industrious they would dig them quickly. Lazy men would clearly take longer to build a wall than industrious ones."

Alice still wasn't convinced. It seemed more like guesswork than arithmetic. "How long is the wall?" she asked. "Surely you need to know that."

"It isn't any length at all. They haven't built it yet," replied the Penguin. "I said how long *would* it take them, not how long *did* it take them."

Alice was none the wiser and asking the Penguin questions was not helping at all. All it was doing was making him cross. She tried to sneak a glance at the Pelican's book. He was writing for all he was worth, dipping his pen in his beak every few seconds. Clearly, he had some idea of how to tackle the problem, but his page was covered with a meaningless jumble of mathematical symbols and formulae. Alice couldn't understand it at all. It certainly didn't seem to have anything to do with men building walls.

"Psst!" she hissed quietly to the Pelican, repeating the sound more loudly louder when he failed to take any notice. The second time he looked up. "How are you working it out?" she asked. "I don't understand the problem at all."

"It's quite easy really," replied the Pelican. As he talked, the ink in his bill spluttered and a few drops splashed onto the floor. "What you've got to realize is the men must have been digging the holes for a reason. Let us assume they were going to plant trees. All trees have roots, and these trees could have square ones. The square root of tree is much the same as the square root of three—it was three men after all..."

"Hush!" the Penguin's shout stopped the Pelican's explanation. "No talking in class. You must try to work this out on your own."

Alice was almost relieved. The Pelican's explanation was even sillier than the original question. Alice wasn't sure who was madder, the teacher or the pupil. It also struck her that even if she did know how to tackle the problem, she had no exercise book anyway. Instead, she stared intently at the desk and tried to look as if she were thinking hard, which indeed she was, but more about how to escape from this lunatic class than about digging holes or building walls.

After a few moments, the teacher's voice interrupted her thoughts. "Right, pass your exercise books to the front. I shall mark them later. It is now time for some English. Take out your English exercise books. I am going to recite a poem. Afterwards I shall expect you to write a short appreciation."

Again, the noise of desks rose to a crescendo and, again, Alice opened hers so as not to appear out of line. The geography book was still there, but there seemed to be something else beneath it. Alice moved the top book to uncover a small green exercise book with *Arithmetic: Class Work* written in rather untidy hand on the front cover. "Why does everything seem to turn up just slightly too late?" wondered Alice.

Alice flicked through the book. None of the pages had been written on, so Alice took it out, thinking she could cross out *Arithmetic* and write *English* in its place. It was only after she had done this she remembered she had no pen. Nothing was going right in class to-day.

The Penguin began to recite:

> *"If only pigs had wings they could*
> *Just fly around all day.*
> *Over hill and dale and wood,*
> *A-grunting on their way.*

If only pigs had wings, I say:
They wouldn't need their hoofs,
And lest the pigs should fly away,
All pigpens would need roofs.

If only pigs had wings, poor things,
On market afternoons,
We'd have to tie them down with strings
Like great big pink balloons.

If only pigs had wings, I thought
That ham might be less salty.
You'd need a net to capture pork,
And bacon would be poultry."

He paused for several seconds as if in a trance, before addressing the class once more. "A fine piece of poetry, I am sure you will all agree. My own work, of course. Now, will you all please write me one and a half pages on the literary merits, hidden meanings, and significance of the subtext."

Alice felt the Penguin ought to have been a little more modest about his own poem. It did not seem at all meaningful to her. If anything, it was a little bit silly. She certainly couldn't think of enough to say about it to fill a page and a half—even if she had *had* a pen.

The Pelican was again writing for all he was worth and most of the other pupils were doing the same. Just then there was a loud crack. The Lobster had been holding its pen too tightly in its powerful claw and had snipped it neatly in half. Grumbling under its breath, it opened its desk, took out another, and continued with its work.

The only one not writing (apart from Alice) was the Seagull. He was frowning and chewing the end of his pen, staring anxiously around the room as if seeking inspiration.

To Alice's immense relief, it was at that moment the school bell rang again. Instantly, the entire class started opening their desks, scraping their chairs, and generally making a noise. Some of them even left their seats and started to make for the door. The Penguin raised his voice, trying desperately to make himself heard above the din. "All right class, finish your appreciation after luncheon. It is now games time."

Alice rose, followed the other pupils out of the class, and off down the corridor. At the end of the passage, some French windows led her and the other students out onto the games field.

Outside another teacher was waiting. This one was an Albatross. He was dressed in white flannel trousers and had a cricket jumper knotted round his neck. Alice couldn't help wondering if he always wore it like that. The sleeves didn't look to be at all large enough for the bird's enormous wings.

"Hello there." The Albatross was addressing Alice. "You're a new girl aren't you? Which games option are you taking this term, cricket or nine men's morris?"

Alice was slightly perplexed. "I thought nine men's morris was a board game."

"Not always," replied the Albatross. "Look over there." He pointed to a far corner of the games field where some pupils were already limbering up. Each was dressed in a traditional morris dancer's white shirt and trousers with bright blue sashes. They had bells strapped to their arms and legs (or in some cases to their wings or paws).

Alice thought it best not to choose that option. She had never seen morris dancing treated as a sport before and had no idea what rules there might be. Besides, there were already nine of them and somehow she felt that might be the ideal number for a team.

"Do you think I could have a try at cricket?" she asked.

"Certainly not," said the Albatross rather abruptly. "You only get *tries* at rugby. Come this way, I think we had better teach you the rules."

So saying he set off in the opposite direction to that of the morris dancers and Alice followed.

Shortly they arrived at the cricket pitch. A number of pupils were already there, including the Lobster and the Pelican. The Lobster had several cricket balls clutched in his claw, and was deftly tossing them, one at a time, to the Pelican who was catching them in his beak. The Pelican hadn't washed his mouth out since class, and each shiny red cricket ball he caught came out again covered in black ink.

There was also another creature, the like of which Alice had never seen before. It stood on six legs, looking rather like an enormous grasshopper. It had wings but, unlike a grasshopper, the wings were thick, black, and leathery. Its body was covered in soft brown fur, and it had a face that reminded her of a small fox.

"Why are you staring at me like that?" asked the creature. "Don't you know it's rude to stare?"

"I'm awfully sorry," Alice said apologetically. "It's just that I have never seen a creature quite like you before."

"That's because I am unique," said the creature proudly. "A cross-breed."

"Are you some sort of sea creature?" asked Alice rather doubtfully. "You don't look as if you are but most of the others at this school seem to be."

"Well, I'm not," said the creature. "Neither am I a pupil at this school. I am here to teach games. You see, I am a cross between a Bat and a Cricket, which makes me a Cricket-Bat."

Alice looked at the creature for a long while.

Then the Albatross called the cricket players to order and started to direct them to their fielding positions. "Now then, young lady," he said, turning to Alice, "I think we'll put you at deep rounded square leg off."

"I'm sorry," said Alice hesitantly, having no idea what he meant.

"No need to be sorry. You've done nothing wrong," the Albatross reassured her.

"I'm afraid I don't understand where I am supposed to go."

"I don't understand you," said the Albatross. "First you are sorry, now you are afraid. There really is nothing to be frightened of. Just go and stand there on that clump of daisies." He pointed to a small patch of flowers some distance away.

Dutifully, Alice walked over to the daisies. By now, all the other fielders had taken their positions and the Lobster was preparing to bowl. A small Duck was standing at the wicket, holding a somewhat over-sized bat rather awkwardly in his beak. The Lobster came in and bowled the first ball. Despite his small stature, the Duck swung his bat with a deftness that surprised Alice. He gave the ball a mighty crack straight in her direction.

"CATCH!" yelled all the fielders in unison.

Alice reached as high as she could, but the ball was just slightly too high for her. It brushed her fingertips and fell to the ground behind her. The fieldsmen groaned disapprovingly as Alice picked up the ball, a little embarrassed, and threw it back. Meanwhile, the Duck had taken a single run and his partner, a Swan, had arrived at the striking end.

The Albatross shouted across to Alice "I think you had better stand a bit further back."

Alice move back a few yards.

"A bit more," shouted the Albatross.

Alice obeyed, but she was getting so far away from the stumps that she was having severe doubts about her ability to throw the ball back should it come to her again.

The Lobster moved in to bowl its second. Another almighty crack ensued. Not altogether surprisingly, the Swan was considerably more powerful than the Duck and yet again the ball came straight towards Alice.

"CATCH!" went up the cry, even louder than before, but the same thing happened. Even running back a little and jumping at the last moment, she could do no more than get her fingers to it. The ball fell to the ground. The other fielders started to murmur angrily and some gave Alice some very black looks. She threw the ball back as hard as she could, but it didn't make it all the way to the wicket. A Turtle, who was fielding closer in, had to collect it and throw it the rest of the way. In the delay, the batsmen managed to take two further runs.

"Further back!" yelled the Albatross.

"If I go any further back, I sha'n't be able to throw the ball in!" Alice shouted back.

"Never mind," shouted the Albatross. "Just throw it to the Turtle. He'll throw it the rest of the way."

Slightly despondently, Alice moved back again. She was starting to feel as if she didn't belong in this game. Everyone else seemed so far away. She was also wondering why the batsmen always seemed to hit the ball at her.

The third ball was bowled. This time the Swan excelled himself and yet again the ball sailed over Alice's head. Some of the other players were looking decidedly angry. Alice felt like shouting that it wasn't her fault. She was doing her best! She picked up the ball sullenly and threw it to the Turtle. She only just managed to get it to him.

"Back some more," yelled the Albatross. Alice obeyed. "Not enough, further!" He had now resorted to using a speaking-trumpet but, even so, Alice could only just make out what he was saying, he was so far away. In fact, some of the other players were now so distant she could hardly see them. Indeed, Alice got the strange impression that not only was she moving back, but the cricket pitch itself was stretching.

From then on, Alice ceased to have any further part in the game. The next ball was not struck in her direction, and the rest of the players had lost interest in her. The wicket was getting further and further away by the minute, even though Alice was not moving. She could no longer hear, and could hardly see, what was going on. It seemed rather pointless her staying there any longer.

Alice turned to discover she was now right on the edge of the field and there were some bushes and a lightly-wooded area not ten feet away. She glanced back toward the cricket pitch, but the game was now so far away she could scarcely make out the individual players.

Alice quickly ran towards the wood and ducked behind the nearest bush.

Once again, she looked back to the cricket pitch to see if anyone had noticed her departure, but she could no longer see anyone at all, so she turned back and set off into the woods.

CHAPTER VI

A Caddy for the King

After such a busy time at the school, Alice was pleased to be on her own for a while. The wood was not nearly so dense and imposing as the one in which she had become lost on her first arrival. The sun filtered down through the trees, making it seem a warm and friendly place.

As she walked, she gathered wild flowers. A few she recognized—like snowdrops and primroses, but others she had never seen before. There was a large orange and blue one, bell-shaped, and Alice had never encountered anything like it. When she sniffed it, she was somewhat surprised to discover it smelled of burnt toast. Another one had delicately pointed petals coloured with pink and green checks. That one smelled of fried sausages and furniture polish.

Rather unwisely, she tried tasting the pink and green one but spat it out again hurriedly. Although slightly peppermint (with undertones of tomato sauce), it tasted mainly of mustard with horseradish relish.

She was about to set off again when she was interrupted by a cry coming from just beyond the next bunch of trees. "FORE!"

Alice ran forward to investigate. The trees in question marked the end of the wood, and beyond was a wide alley of open grass, bordered on the far side by more trees and bushes. As she was taking this all in, there was a crash and something hard landed in the bush beside her.

"What on earth was that?" Alice said, rather startled. When something frightened her she always found it best to talk to herself about it. Somehow that made it less worrying.

She peered into the bush to see what it was that had given her such a shock. Pulling the branches aside, the only unusual object she could find was a woodlouse rolled up into a ball—not that woodlice are particularly unusual of course. It was just that this one was so large. It must have been at least two inches across when rolled up.

"Very odd," said Alice. "I ca'n't see anything else in the bush, and one doesn't normally expect to find woodlice flying through the air, not even enormous ones like this. Not that I have much experience of enormous woodlice, mind you. I just don't see why they should be any more likely to fly than normal ones. Probably less so, I should say."

She had just taken it from the bush to have a closer look when she became aware of someone walking towards her. She looked up to see the Red King strolling over, with a golf bag slung over his shoulder.

"Good afternoon young lady," said the King. "I see you have found my ball."

"Isn't it just a little bit cruel," asked Alice, "playing golf with a woodlouse?"

"I never play golf with woodlice," responded the King. "I generally find they are very poor players. I only ever play on my own or with the White King. Would you mind caddying for the rest of this round?"

The King didn't wait for an answer but passed his bag to Alice. She could see why he wanted to get rid of it. It was rather heavy.

"I thought one was only meant to keep golf clubs in a golf bag," said Alice. "This one seems to have all sorts of strange things in it. There's a spade, a pickaxe, even a billiard-cue."

"Must make sure you always have the right tool for the job," replied the King. "Now then, free drop from here, I think." He took the ball from Alice and dropped it on the ground, where it fell behind a clump of grass.

"Isn't that an oak tree?" said the King pointing.

Alice looked round and turned back to tell the King that it was—just in time to see him surreptitiously pushing the ball into a more favourable position with his foot.

"That's the best drive I've had all afternoon," said the King. "Do you see those markers over there? That is where the tee is. It must be all of two hundred yards away and I drove the whole distance in one shot."

He pointed to where some red marker triangles stood, some distance down the grass alley.

"Yes, that is a fair way," agreed Alice.

"Ah. I see you've played this game before," said the King. "Right, I think I'll have my number six iron for this next one please."

Alice looked in the bag. The pickaxe had the number six engraved on it—or maybe it was nine, it depended which way up you looked at it. She handed it to the King and he seemed happy with it.

"Stand back," warned the King. He took a mighty swing, sending the unfortunate woodlouse sailing through the air.

"Not bad, though I say it myself," said the King with some satisfaction. "Come on, I think that one is on the green."

He threw the pickaxe back into the golf bag with such force that it nearly made Alice fall over, and set off in pursuit of his ball.

Alice followed as fast as she could with her heavy burden, but it was impossible to keep up. The King was oblivious to her difficulties and was striding on ahead. It clearly did not occur to him she might not be right behind him, because he was still talking to her in a normal voice.

"I'm sorry," Alice called after him. "You'll have to slow down. I'm dropping behind and I ca'n't hear what you are saying."

The King stopped and turned, and waited for Alice to catch up.

"I can see we shall have to give you some more exercise," he said when she finally arrived. "Not enough stamina."

"It's not that," Alice protested. "It's just that this golf bag is getting rather heavy, there is so much in it."

"I don't see how it can be getting heavy," said the King. "Unless you put more things inside, I tend to find things stay much the same weight. Anyway we're there now."

Sure enough, they had arrived at the green. The King's woodlouse had landed about ten feet from the hole. "Will you take out the flag please?" asked the King.

Alice dropped the bag on the ground, strolled over to the hole, and pulled out the flagstick. The King, meanwhile, had selected the billiard-cue from his golf bag and was crouching on all fours behind his ball. With his chin practically on the ground, he carefully lined up for the shot and, with great skill, neatly potted the ball in the hole. He made it look so simple it made Alice wonder why anyone bothered with proper putting at all.

"Birdie four," exclaimed the King. "Not bad at all. We had better hurry to the clubhouse now. It must be time to get ready for the party."

"What party?" asked Alice.

"Why, the coming-out party of course," replied the King. "Surely you have heard about it. The Jack assured me he had invited everyone."

"You mean *my* party?" asked Alice excitedly. "I never realized the King himself would be invited."

To Alice's immense relief, the King picked up his own golf bag and set off towards the club house, which overlooked the green where they stood. "How very strange," thought Alice. "I never noticed the club house when we arrived. I expect it was there all the time though. Things like houses don't usually creep up on you."

"Yes, my wife, the Queen, is organizing it all," continued the King. Alice was not at all pleased to hear this news. "It's at Oddfellows' Hall this very afternoon. We are to help a young lady called Celia find her way home."

"I think that is me," said Alice, "although my real name is Alice. It is just that the Jack seems rather fond of anagrams."

"Yes he is, rather," agreed the Red King. "He calls me 'kind

Reg', you know. If you are to be the guest of honour, I think it would be most fitting if you would allow me to accompany you to the ball."

"I should be delighted, your Majesty," said Alice, and she gave a little curtsy.

By now, they had arrived at the clubhouse and went inside. "Have you seen my cups?" asked the King, discarding his golf bag on the floor. He pointed to a large display cabinet on the far wall. Alice walked over and looked inside.

"But they're just tea cups," she protested. "I thought one usually received silver cups as golf trophies."

The King looked a little disappointed. "My silversmith assured me they were the most unusual golf trophies I should ever see."

"Oh I'm sure they are," agreed Alice, slightly regretting she had been so critical. "I have certainly never seen trophies like these. You must have won lots of competitions."

"It's because I play on my own a lot," the King explained. "I generally find that when I do that, I win. The large blue one I got for wearing out a pair of socks."

"Why did you get a cup for that?" Alice asked, slightly taken aback.

"To be honest, I don't know," said the King. "My silversmith just happened to be here one afternoon when I returned from a round of golf. I was pulling off my golf shoes and chanced to notice I had snagged one of my socks. I remarked to him (by way of conversation, you understand) 'Oh look, I've got a hole in one,' and he immediately said 'Well done, your Majesty,' and gave me that cup. To this day I ca'n't see why he did it. Anyway, enough of my golfing triumphs. It is time we got ready for this party." He pulled off his golfing shoes and extracted a pair of slippers from under the bench.

"My coach will be here shortly. Tell me, young lady, just what is this plight with which we are supposed to assist you?"

"The truth of the matter is I am lost," Alice explained. "You see, I am not exactly sure how I got here, so I don't know how to get home."

"How come you don't know how you got here?" asked the King. "Did you lose your memory? Very careless that. A lost memory can be very hard to find because you can never remember where you put it."

"No, I haven't lost my memory," Alice assured him. "It's just that I was asleep at the time. I went up to bed, then the next thing I knew was when I woke up in a boat."

"Well, I know which direction you need to go," said the King.

"Really?" asked Alice, thinking help might be at hand at last.

"Yes," replied the King. "You need to go downwards. If you went up to bed and then woke up again, you must be getting very high indeed. I recommend you go down to bed and then see if you ca'n't wake down."

Alice's hopes fell again. The King was no help at all. He was just as mad as everyone else she had met recently.

"Do you hear that?" said the King suddenly. "I think my coach has arrived."

Alice had heard nothing, but the King opened the clubhouse door and there it was, sure enough. Parked outside was a beautiful coach drawn by four snow-white horses. The bodywork was painted shining gold and covered with intricate carvings. At the front, the coach driver sat bolt upright, wearing a red livery trimmed with gold braid, and a powdered wig. Only the fact that he happened to be a pig detracted slightly from his smart appearance. Another pig coachman, similarly attired, was holding the coach door open.

The King strolled out of the clubhouse and climbed the coach steps. The pig doorman bowed low, grunting with the effort of the manoeuvre. Turning to look over his shoulder, the King called back to Alice.

"Come along my girl, we shall be late if you don't hurry."
Alice followed him into the coach.

"Is it far to the hall?" asked Alice, once the coach had set off.

"Not very," replied the King. "It should only take a few minutes. Would you care for a game of darts to pass the time?"

"Wouldn't that be a bit difficult in such a confined space?" asked Alice. "And dangerous too, I shouldn't wonder."

"Not at all," said the King. "We can throw them outside."

He stood up and reached into the luggage rack. From it, he produced a dartboard and some lengths of cane with brass fittings on each end. Alice watched, fascinated, as the King attached the dartboard to the end of one of the canes. He then started to screw the canes together like a chimney sweep's brush.

When the resulting pole became too long for the carriage, the King pushed the dartboard end out through the window. He then continued to add several more sections. By the time he had finished, the dartboard was suspended on the end of his pole, some ten feet or more beyond the carriage window. The cane was fairly flexible, and the dartboard bounced up and down wildly as the carriage ran along the bumpy road.

"You throw first while I hold the pole for you," announced the King, and he produced three darts from his waistcoat pocket and handed them to Alice.

"What if I miss the board all together?" asked Alice. "I'm quite likely to, you know. I'm not very good at darts at the best of times, and the board is moving about rather a lot."

"We can always stop and collect them," replied the King. "Come on, hurry up and have your turn."

Alice was soon proved right. It was a silly idea. Hardly any of her darts hit the board, and the King in his turn wasn't much better. Even on those rare occasions when the darts did manage to stick in the board, things were far from simple. It was then necessary to manoeuvre the back end of the pole out through the opposite window in order to bring the board within reach so the darts could be retrieved. More often than not, the darts fell out of the board as Alice and the King tried to pull it in through the window.

They must have stopped the coach to collect their darts a dozen times or more, and Alice was getting a little fed up. "Don't you think we should stop now?" she pleaded. "If we keep having to stop to collect our darts, I don't suppose we shall ever get to the party."

"Such nonsense, girl," scoffed the King. "Of course we shall get there. But if you would rather play something else, we could put the darts away for a while. How about a game of cricket?"

Alice could not even begin to imagine how the King intended to play cricket within the confines of the coach and felt sure any such idea was doomed to failure. "Do you suppose," she asked, "we could just look at the view for a while?"

"Oh I suppose so, if you insist. Perhaps we could play 'I spy'."

Alice would rather have played nothing at all, but a least "I spy" seemed a more practical suggestion, and a little less energetic. Alice agreed.

"Just help me get the dartboard in, if you don't mind," said the King, and he started to unscrew the poles, handing them to Alice one at a time. All went well until the last. As the King was pulling it in through the window, the dartboard caught on the outside of the window frame.

"Watch out!" Alice shouted, and made a grab for the dartboard. Unfortunately, her armful of canes got in the way and she was too late to prevent the board from tumbling down outside the coach.

"Quick, after it!" shouted the King, as he banged on the wall to make the coachman stop the carriage yet again. "That is my best dartboard. If I lose it, the Queen will never buy me another."

Alice jumped down from the coach. Being round, the dartboard was rolling away down the road and Alice set off in pursuit. She had almost caught up with it when a noise made her spin round. The coach had started to move off again.

"Hey, wait for me!" she shouted, but in vain. "What about your dartboard?" Alas, the coach was already too far away for her shouts to be heard above the rumbling of the wheels on the road. All she could do was stand and watch it as it went off into the distance.

"Well, really," said Alice. "I hope the Queen gives him a thorough scolding for losing his dartboard. It would serve him right for setting off without me."

She turned again just in time to see the dartboard, which had rolled on another few yards, come to a halt and fall flat on the ground. "I suppose if I collect it and return it to its rightful owner I might even get a reward. Kings give exceedingly good rewards when people do nice things for them, or so I am told. If only I can find this Oddfellows' Hall so I can give it to him."

As she approached the dartboard, something struck her as a little odd.

"I'm sure, when we were playing, the dartboard had yellow parts as well as black. I ca'n't see any yellow at all now. In fact, it looks so black that it looks more like a hole in the road than a dartboard." She stepped a bit closer and peered at the dartboard more carefully.

Sure enough, there, at her feet, was a perfectly round hole. Alice got down on all fours to have a closer look. "There seems to be a ladder inside. I suppose that means it must lead somewhere."

Yet again, Alice's curiosity got the better of her. "I don't suppose it would matter to have a quick look. If there is nothing very interesting down there, or if it is at all frightening, I could always climb out again."

Having thus reassured herself, Alice started to descend the ladder.

CHAPTER VII

At Home Underground

*I*t was extremely dark inside the hole. Alice could only just make out the rungs of the ladder as she descended in the gloom. It *was* a little bit frightening so she started to talk to herself, just to keep herself company. "I do wish there weren't so many cobwebs. They keep getting tangled round my fingers and in my hair. I wonder why spiders' webs are called cobwebs. Do you suppose spiders used to be called 'cobs' once upon a time? This ladder seems to be going on forever. I do hope it leads somewhere."

Suddenly, and without any warning, the ladder came to an end. Alice put her foot down onto what should have been the next rung but it wasn't there. With a cry of anguish, she fell about four feet, landing slightly uncomfortably, but uninjured, in a pile of pots and pans.

"What a strange thing to find at the bottom of a hole," Alice remarked, a little shaken. "I wonder what all these pots are doing here."

"They aren't doing anything," said a voice from the darkness, making Alice jump. "At least they weren't until you arrived. Then some of them started to fall down. Pity. It was a nice neat pile."

"Who's that?" asked Alice. "Who is there?"

"Me," said the voice.

"That doesn't help at all," said Alice. "If I ca'n't see you, how do I know who 'me' is?"

"What terrible grammar," the voice chastised. "You don't say 'How do I know who *me is*?'; you say 'How do I know who *I am*?'."

"That's not what I meant at all," protested Alice. "I meant how am I supposed to know who *you* are when I ca'n't see you because it is too dark?"

"Would it help if I were a bit lighter?" asked the voice.

"I suppose it might," Alice replied, slightly doubtfully.

"Then I had better go on a diet," the voice said.

"This conversation is getting us nowhere," protested Alice.

"No," sighed the voice wistfully. "That seems to be the way of conversations. I generally find trains and busses better for getting you somewhere."

Alice was becoming exasperated. "I mean if you diet it makes you lighter in weight, not lighter in colour. If you went on a diet, you would just be thinner and even more difficult to see."

"Sometimes you diet to make things lighter in colour," said the voice.

"Well, I have never heard of such a thing," replied Alice.

"If you want your hair to be a lighter colour you can dye it," explained the voice.

Alice was about to protest that this was spelt differently but, at that moment, her companion struck a match. In the flare, Alice could finally see she was talking to a large Mole with black fur. In his left hand, he held a small candle on a stand and this he now lit. As the flame gathered strength, Alice was able to survey the scene more clearly. She was in a small dusty room with tunnels leading off in just about every direction. The Mole had just put on a pair of heavy rimmed spectacles and was peering, short-sightedly, at Alice with a questioning look on his face.

"What sort of creature are you?" he finally asked. "You don't look much like a mole or a worm, or any of the other sorts of creatures one generally meets underground."

"I am a girl," replied Alice.

"What's that?" asked the Mole in an incredulous tone, taking a step backwards. "You mean a human girl? You ca'n't be. You're much too small for one thing."

"I am not at all," said Alice indignantly. "I am just the right size. Come to think of it, you are rather large for a mole."

"Not in the least," said the Mole, just as indignantly. "There's nothing wrong with my size. It's you that's the wrong size. Why, you ca'n't be more than nine inches from top to bottom—or maybe ten from bottom to top. Are you sure you didn't shrink as you came down the hole?"

"No. At least I don't think so." By now, Alice was losing her confidence. The Mole was about the same size as herself and past experience of girls and moles did indicate that girls, even little ones, were invariably much the larger. But it was slowly dawning on her that she had no means of telling which of the two of them was either too large *or* too small.

Suddenly, she had a bright idea.

"If I had been shrinking as I came down the hole, the ladder would have seemed to get wider and the rungs would have got thicker and further apart," she announced triumphantly. "They didn't. It stayed the same all the way down."

"Well, that just proves you were shrinking." said the Mole, with a self-righteous sort of sniff. "You only have to stand at the top of any tall ladder and look down it, to see it is much narrower at the bottom than it is at the top. If it seemed to stay the same, you must have been shrinking."

"But if you stood at the bottom and looked up," Alice pointed out, "wouldn't it then look wider at the bottom than at the top?"

"I dare say," responded the Mole, "but you came down the ladder, not up it."

"What about these pans?" asked Alice, changing tack. "If I were only nine inches tall, the pots and pans would be as big as me. They aren't. They are just the right size."

"That proves nothing," replied the Mole. "How do you know these pots and pans are the same size as the ones you are used to?"

Alice had to admit defeat. It occurred to her that, for all she knew, she might be a different size every time she woke up in the morning. So long as everything and everyone else changed in proportion, she could never know. She decided to change the subject and return to her original question. "Why are all those pots here anyway? I could have hurt myself landing on those."

"Those are my pots, and I keep them here because this is my pot hole." explained the Mole. "But enough of them. Who are you, why are you here, and where are you going?"

"My name is Alice, and I'm trying to get to the coming-out ball."

"You mean you are the little girl who is trying to find her way home?"

"Yes," Alice replied. It was rather flattering the way everyone seemed to have heard of her difficulties. It made her feel quite important. "I don't suppose you could tell me how to get to Oddfellows' Hall?"

"I understand there are going to be party games," said the Mole. ("Ignoring people's questions seems to be an annoyingly common habit amongst the inhabitants of this strange land," thought Alice.) "Were you playing golf?"

This question came as a surprise to Alice, since it had, so far as she could tell, nothing at all to do with the preceding conversation. "Not actually playing, you understand. I was caddying for the King."

"Oh," said the Mole, sounding slightly disappointed. "It's just that if you had been playing, it might have explained how you came to be in my pot hole. You might have turned into a golf ball and been holed."

"People don't just turn into golf balls," said Alice, but even as she spoke, she remembered the Red Queen's croquet game. Perhaps it wasn't as impossible as it sounded. A lot of very odd things did seem to have happened recently.

"They do, you know," continued the Mole. "People turn into all sorts of things. Caterpillars turn into butterflies, coaches turn into drive-ways, children turn into grown ups, all for no apparent reason whatsoever. Why, only last week I turned into a mole. Imagine that."

"That's not the same sort of thing at all. Children are meant to turn into grown ups—that's what growing up means. I must admit, though, turning into a mole is somewhat remarkable. What were you before you turned into one?"

"I don't rightly recall," answered the Mole with a sigh. "It seems such a long time ago."

Alice was certain that if anything as dramatic as changing into a mole ever happened to her, she would remember it quite distinctly. She certainly could not imagine ever forgetting she had once been a little girl but she decided not to press the point. Instead, she asked the Mole once more whether he was aware of the correct route to Oddfellows' Hall.

"Yes, of course," replied the Mole rather curtly. "Follow me."

Without further warning, he darted off down one of the tunnels. Alice had to run after him for fear of losing him.

"Do you know any good walking rhymes?" asked the Mole when she finally caught up.

"I don't think so," panted Alice. 'I'm not sure what a walking rhyme is…. Er, do you think we might slow down a little?"

The Mole slowed down to a brisk march. "It's a rhyme you say when you are walking, of course. It helps to pass the time."

"I've never heard of such a thing," said Alice.

"You're remarkably ignorant, even for a human being," said the Mole. "Never mind. I know a good one:

> *"There was twice a mole,*
> *Went for a stroll,*
> *Along a hole."*

"What do you mean 'There was twice a mole'?" asked Alice.

"It's like saying 'There was once a mole', only it happened more than once," replied the Mole. 'Now don't interrupt.

> *"There was twice a mole,*
> *Went for a stroll,*
> *Along a hole.*
>
> *Underground,*
> *Without a sound*
> *He wandered round,*
>
> *Looking for*
> *The golden door*
> *Which he was sure*
>
> *Concealed the way,*
> *Which he did pray*
> *He'd find that day.*

For he'd been told
This door of rolled
And hammered gold

Would lead onto
The tunnel through
Which me and you

And creatures all
Get to the ball
At Oddfellows' Hall.

So he strode along,
Singing this song.

"No, this is wrong."

At first, Alice thought the last sentence was part of the rhyme. Then she realized the reason for the Mole's comment. They had arrived back in the dusty room from which they had set out.

"I don't think you know where you are going at all," declared Alice. "We've just gone round in a circle."

"How do you know?" snapped the Mole. "It might have been a square, or an oval."

"That's not the point," protested Alice. "The fact is we've been walking for several minutes and got nowhere."

"I don't think this is nowhere," said the Mole. "I've been here several times before and I'm sure it is somewhere. Now come on, or we shall be late for the ball. This tunnel leads to the golden door."

He set off again, down a different tunnel this time. Again, Alice followed but it was no use. It seemed like hardly any time at all before they were back in the room full of pots and pans.

"I don't think any of these tunnels lead anywhere," said Alice in despair. "Are you sure you know where you are going?"

"Quite sure, quite sure," muttered the Mole. "Just follow me," and he set off down yet another of the tunnels. But Alice had had enough. She waited until the Mole was out of sight, and then turned and set off down a different tunnel in the opposite direction.

It was difficult to see where she was going without the help of the Mole's candle but, fortunately, the corridor wasn't in total darkness. At regular intervals along the wall, small and somewhat inefficient gas lamps produced just about enough light for Alice to make her way. After only a few hundred yards of twisting and turning in the gloom, the tunnel abruptly came to an end at a huge, beautifully polished and shining golden door. Even in the gloomy light, the metal surface twinkled, almost as if it were winking at her.

"What a very curious thing to find in an underground tunnel, to be sure," said Alice, rather overawed. "I wonder if the Mole was right, and this really is the way to Oddfellows' Hall."

The door must have been all of fifteen feet high and the handle was rather a long way up. Apart from its size, and the shining gold metal from which it was made, it looked almost identical to Alice's own front door at home. Alice stood on tiptoe but she could only just reach the handle with the tips of her fingers. There was no hope of her actually turning it. She tried jumping to reach it a few times, but it was hopeless.

"What am I to do?" wondered Alice. "Will I ever get out of these tunnels again? Why did that silly Mole have to keep going the wrong way? If we had found the door together, I could have sat on his shoulders to open it—if moles have shoulders, that is. I'm not at all sure they do. Anyway, I suppose he could have sat on my shoulders if not."

She gave the door a kick but it only made her toes hurt. Alice sat down and cradled her head in her hands. She was beginning to wonder if she was destined to spend the rest of her days in her underground prison, and whether she was doomed to starve, or whether all those pots and pans meant there was a supply of food nearby—possibly even a kitchen. Then she had an idea. "I suppose if I went back and fetched a few of those pots and pans, I might be able to reach the door handle if I stood on them."

Alice ran back down the tunnel to the little room and collected as many of the largest saucepans as she could carry. Then, moving awkwardly through the narrow tunnel with all her baggage, she set off back towards the door.

Only after several minutes' walking did she realize something was wrong.

"I'm sure I should have found the door by now," she said, a little distressed. "Where has it got to? I am certain this is the same tunnel, so where on earth is the door? Or," added Alice, remembering what the oak tree had said to her, "where *in* earth is it?"

She kept going for another few minutes but it was becoming increasingly apparent the door was nowhere to be found. The tunnel was slightly wider now and Alice was sure she hadn't passed this way before. After a few more twists and turns, the tunnel came to a dead end.

"Bother!" shouted Alice. In a fit of temper she hurled her largest saucepan at the end wall. The force of the impact must have dislodged something, causing a great quantity of earth and dust to fall from the ceiling, all over Alice. She coughed and spluttered, but as the dust subsided she saw something that gave her fresh hope—there was a faint glimmer of daylight coming from above.

Her hopes were short-lived. She soon found the tunnel was much too tall for her to reach the ceiling to pull herself up, even standing on the pans.

"No. I mustn't cry," said Alice, bravely fighting back the tears. "While there's life there's hope. That's what my sister always says. If only she were here now. I'm sure she would know what to do. Mind you, I suppose even if *she* isn't around, someone might be." She took a deep breath.

"*Help!*" shouted Alice at the top of her voice, but to no avail. Then she picked up two of the saucepans and banged them together with all her might until her ears ached. "HELP!" she yelled again.

Then came a sound like music to Alice's ringing ears—a voice from above, with a strong country accent. "Who's that? Who's there? Bless my soul, 'tis a talkin' tree stump."

"It's not a talking tree stump at all. I'm down here!" called Alice, hoarse from her shouting.

"All I can see is this 'ere old 'ollow tree stump with an 'ole in 'un. You're inside, eh?"

"Yes, I suppose so. Do you think you might be able to make the hole a bit bigger, so I can get out?"

"Can't say as I know," said the voice, "but I'll 'ave a go any'ow."

The voice was replaced by a great deal of grunting and straining. This was followed by a loud tearing sound, and a good deal more soil tumbled down onto Alice. When she finally opened her eyes again, a great sense of relief came over her. Sunlight was pouring in through what was now a large hole in the roof, and peering in through the hole was the beaming and bearded face of her rescuer.

"'Old on, miss, I'll get you somethin' to climb out on," said the face. It vanished, but returned a few moments later and a large branch was lowered into the hole. The branch had several smaller branches sticking out at regular intervals all the way along. It could almost have been made as a ladder. Alice was easily able to climb out, and she collapsed with relief onto the warm grass.

"Hallo there," said her rescuer. "I be the Red King's game-keeper. Who might you be?"

"Alice," replied Alice, wondering if he too had heard of her and her plight.

"Oh. And who are you then?"

"I just told you, I am Alice," repeated Alice, a little curtly.

"I was just wantin' to be sure, you understand," apologized the gamekeeper. "Seein' as 'ow I only axed who you might be. I thought I'd better ax who you actually was. What was you a-doin' of down that ol' tree stump?"

"It's rather a long story," replied Alice. "All I really want to do is find my way to Oddfellows' Hall. Do you think you could take me?"

"I do believe as I can," replied the gamekeeper. "I be goin' that way now, mysel'. Why don't you walk along wi' me, and we'll go there together."

Gratefully, Alice accepted the invitation. The two set off together, the gamekeeper whistling softly as they went.

CHAPTER VIII

Fox and Geese

As they strolled on in the sunshine, the gamekeeper seemed reluctant to indulge in further conversation so Alice contented herself with taking stock of her companion. His beard was longer than she had thought at first sight, and he kept running his fingers through it as they walked. It was as if he were trying to tease it out little by little. Had Alice not known better, she would have said he was succeeding. It seemed to be growing longer by the minute.

His clothes were a little dishevelled and bore the signs of having been well worn. From the top pocket of his jacket protruded several playing cards while a chess-board, folded with the squares outermost, stuck out at a jaunty angle from the bag slung over his shoulder.

"Why do you carry a chess-board?" asked Alice eventually, growing tired of the long silence. "Do you ever have a chance to stop for a game while you are out in the woods?"

"I told you, I be the King's gamekeeper," he responded.

"I thought gamekeepers generally had to look after wild life and chase off poachers."

"Well, well, I never 'eard the like," replied the gamekeeper, tugging again at his beard and producing (or so it seemed) yet another inch or two of growth. "I jes' look after 'is Majesty's games. See 'ere. I keep 'is dominoes in one pocket and 'is spare dice in t'other. I do look after 'is fox and the geese though. I s'pose you could call *them* wild life."

For some reason, beyond Alice for the moment, the game-keeper dropped to his knees and proceeded to crawl along on all fours.

Presently they arrived at a fence to which was attached a large notice reading "TRESPASSERS KEEP OUT."

"Oh dear," exclaimed Alice. "Are we allowed to go this way?"

"Don't apply to us, does it?" grunted the gamekeeper. "We ain't gone in yet, so we ca'n't be no trespassers. This 'ere notice only applies to trespassers." So saying, he shuffled up to the fence, took a bite out of a lump of grass growing near one of the fence posts, and started to munch it thoughtfully.

He really was beginning to behave very strangely. Alice wondered what an earth he might do next. "If we went in, we might *be* trespassers."

"Wouldn't matter if we was," said the gamekeeper. "By that time t'would be too late. We'd already be in, so we couldn't keep out, could we?"

His logic was undeniable and Alice wondered what use such a notice could ever be. The gamekeeper was now rubbing his side up and down the fence post as if trying to relieve an itch. He looked so helpless that Alice reached out and helped to scratch the offending area. The tweed of his jacket felt strange to her—oddly furry.

"I think it is most inconsiderate of you, turning into a goat before we have even finished our conversation," said Alice indignantly. "Does Oddfellows' Hall lie this way, across the field?"

Alas, the goat appeared unable to talk, merely bleating at her pathetically and then munching another mouthful of grass. Indeed, the only evidence it had ever been anything *but* a goat was the fact that it still wore the gamekeeper's hat and satchel.

"You might at *least* have remained a gamekeeper long enough to set me off in the right direction," Alice complained. "Everyone I meet seems to want to help me at first but nothing ever comes of it. Why, I shouldn't be surprised if you changed

into a goat on purpose just so you didn't have to take me all the way to the hall!"

The goat bleated again then bit a large lump out of its satchel, chewing it with apparent relish.

"Well, there seems to be little point in remaining here trying to get any further sense from you. All you want to do is eat." The goat had shaken the hat from its head and taken it into its mouth whole, making its cheeks bulge.

"I suppose I shall have to find my own way again. Well, this way seems as good as any other. I shall wish you good day." Alice curtsied politely, then clambered over the fence and set off across the lightly-wooded terrain that lay beyond.

She had not been walking for long when she became aware of a terrible commotion somewhere ahead—a great deal of hooting and the sound of something running. A few moments later, a Fox burst through the undergrowth giving Alice a considerable fright.

"I do beg your pardon young lady," said the Fox, a bit flustered. "I didn't mean to startle you. It's just that those Geese are after me. I thought I could break through to get to the hall, but they formed a line and nearly had me surrounded. I should watch your step, if I were you, lest they get you too. Good day."

He bent his front legs slightly in semblance of a polite bow and set off once more. Alice scarcely had time to take in his warning before the Geese broke through the bushes. There were four of them, side by side, looking for all the world like a rank of soldiers. Before she had time to escape, they spread out and surrounded her against a bush.

"Ha!" (or was it "Honk!"?) went the second from the left. "What shall we do with this one?"

"Take her by the left leg and throw her down the stairs," responded the leftmost.

"I think that's a waste," objected the third Goose. "I think we should fatten her up for Christmas."

"You should do nothing of the sort," interjected Alice. "I have no intention of letting you eat me for Christmas."

"Perish the thought, perish the thought," squawked the fourth Goose.

"It gives me goose pimples just to think of it," interrupted the first Goose.

"No," continued the fourth Goose. "We only eat gooseberries. It's just that if we fatten you up, you will be much too full at Christmas to eat any of us."

"Indeed so," murmured the others solemnly.

"Really, I mean you no harm at all," Alice assured them. "All I want to do is find my way to Oddfellows' Hall. If you'll just let me pass, I promise not to eat any of you."

"Well, I don't know," said the second Goose. "What do you think brothers, do we let her pass and see if we ca'n't catch that terrible Fox?"

"Perhaps if she answers a riddle," suggested the third Goose. "There's a man and a goose at the top of a very tall tower. How does the man get down?"

"I really have no idea," confessed Alice. "Are there no stairs?"

"That's no sort of an answer," replied the third Goose. "What sort of a riddle would it be if he could just walk down the stairs? No. The man can get down by plucking the goose."

"How can you suggest such a thing?" protested the first Goose. "Pluck the goose. What a horrid suggestion."

"It was only a riddle," the third Goose reassured him. "No one's really going to be plucked. Don't be such a silly g—"

"She didn't answer the riddle," interrupted the second Goose. "Does that mean we don't let her go?"

"She can go if she tells us a rhyme," replied the fourth Goose.

"Yes," agreed the first Goose. "She must tell us a rhyme—an animal rhyme, then she can go."

In the heat of the moment, Alice could only think of one animal rhyme, so she began to sing, a bit nervously:

"Goosey goosey gander, whither shall I wander?
Upstairs and—"

"Oh, I know this one," interrupted the third Goose, and he picked up where Alice had left off:

"Upstairs and downstairs and in my lady's chamber.
There I met the pieman who sells at local fairs,
And said 'Kind sir, I beg you, please let me taste your wares.'"

"No, that's not at all right," protested Alice. "You've got the ending muddled up with Simple Simon."

"Not at all," said the third Goose indignantly. "I'm a goose. I should know."

"Anyway, it's not a very good rhyme," said the first Goose, a little pompously. "I thought you looked the sort to tell a really good animal rhyme."

"I'm very sorry," replied Alice. "But I'm afraid it's the only animal rhyme I can think of right now."

"You wait," said the third Goose excitedly. "My brother knows a really good one about a zoo."

"Yes, mine is much better," continued the first Goose. "Just listen young lady, and you might learn something. He cleared his throat with a rasping honk, and began:

"The lion was telling the truth
When he said he'd a pain in his tooth,
But the lion was lyin'
When he said he was dyin',
So no one believed the poor youth."

"I know the next verse," piped up the third Goose again, his excitement growing by the minute. "Please let me tell it brother, please."

"Oh very well," said the first Goose a little gruffly. He folded his wings and turned his back on the others, as if sulking because someone else was stealing the limelight.

This display of temper did not dampen the third Goose's enthusiasm and he launched eagerly into the next couple of verses:

> *"The teacher at animal school*
> *Was, sadly, a little bit cruel.*
> *So the pupils would chorus:*
> *"The Tortoise who taught us*
> *Was much better liked as a rule."*

> *The Antelope loves Annie Ant.*
> *They so want to marry, but ca'n't.*
> *So this Antelope beau*
> *And his Ant eloped so*
> *Now they live with their friend Ellie Phant."*

"You've told enough now," the fourth Goose interrupted. "It's my turn for a verse."

The third Goose tried to protest, but the fourth Goose started to recite loudly, drowning his objections.

> *"A friar of rather large size*
> *Won a trip to the zoo as a prize.*
> *When the young monkey saw*
> *The fat monk 'e swore*
> *It was really the bear in disguise."*

"My turn now you two," honked the second Goose. The other geese (including the first Goose, who had turned back to face the others again) glared at him, but he seemed oblivious.

"The well-mannered young chimpanzee
Said 'Rhinoceros, please stay to tea.'
'Oh, I must say good-bye. No,'
Said rhino, 'For I know
My mum will be waiting for me.'"

"My turn," said the third Goose shrilly.

"Nonsense," shouted the fourth Goose. "You've already told two verses, and I've only said one. It's my turn."

"I haven't said one for ages," said the first Goose. "It must be my turn."

"No, it's not," said the second Goose petulantly. "I want to tell another verse. He told two," (he pointed a wing accusingly at the third Goose) "so it's only fair I should."

"No, you don't," honked the first Goose angrily, and he gave the second Goose (who was much smaller than he was) a shove into a nearby bush.

"You big bully!" shrieked the third Goose. "Take that!" and he pecked him on the neck.

The first Goose started to wave his wings angrily and Alice thought he was about to clip the third Goose round the ear. At that moment the fourth Goose joined in the fray and pecked a large lump of down from the first Goose's chest.

It was clear the fight could only get worse. The second Goose had already picked himself up and was dusting himself off. He looked as if he wanted to get back into the battle. None of the geese were paying Alice any attention any more so she quietly edged her way round the bush. Once out of sight of the geese, she set off at a brisk trot, as the sound of honking and squawking rose to a crescendo. Looking over her shoulder, she could see feathers flying in the air above the bush.

"I think I escaped in the nick of time," thought Alice. "They really were the worst-tempered geese I've met in a long time. Mind you, now I come to think about it, I don't recall ever having met any good-tempered geese."

Already the sound of the battling geese was fading. Soon she could hear it no more, so Alice slowed down to a more restful pace.

CHAPTER IX

Cow and Cable-Car

*I*t had been such a lovely day that Alice was rather surprised when she thought she saw the odd snowflake in the air.

"There's another one!" she exclaimed. "It seems to be snowing—yet there's not a cloud in the sky and the sun is still shining. But wait now—I do believe those aren't snowflakes at all. They look more like cherry blossom petals!"

But cherry blossom petals seemed to make as little sense as did snow. Alice had left the last of the trees behind several minutes ago and was now walking across open scrubland, covered with bracken and heathers. There wasn't a cherry tree in sight, nor any other sort of tree for that matter.

The petals were falling thick and fast now, catching in her hair and in the folds of her dress. "I wish I had an umbrella," moaned Alice. "I never realized how unpleasant it was, getting caught in a petal shower."

By now, the petals were pouring down. A light breeze had started to whip the shower into a blizzard and it was getting harder and harder to see. Alice broke into a trot, then into a run, hoping soon to find some shelter. She was panting with the exertion, with the result that petals got into her mouth. She spat them out and wiped the petals from her face. Petals were swirling in front of her eyes so she could see no more than a few feet ahead. Snowdrifts of petals were building up on the ground and it was difficult to make headway.

Then, almost as suddenly as it had started, the blizzard stopped. Alice wiped the last of the petals from her eyes and stared around. The storm had changed the landscape completely. No longer was there any undergrowth, just a sea of white petals as far as the eye could see. The ground was not as flat as it had been either. There was a definite slope to it.

"I seem to be on a mountain side," said Alice. "Indeed, I do believe I can hear cowbells in the distance."

As the air cleared of petals, she could make out further mountain peaks in the distance. The tinkling of the cowbells was getting louder. Then a sudden swishing noise made Alice spin round just in time to see a large black and white Cow glide skilfully up to where she was standing —a short ski attached to each of the Cow's four legs. "Oh!" cried Alice, somewhat taken aback.

When she had recovered her composure, she continued, "I don't suppose you could tell me whether I'm going the right way for Oddfellows' Hall?"

"Moo," replied the Cow, rather to Alice's disappointment.

"If you're clever enough to ski, surely you must be clever enough to talk," said Alice.

"Moo," repeated the Cow, then she set off again skiing down the slope and was soon lost to view.

"Well, *she* was a lot of help," said Alice dryly. "There seems to be little point staying here. I wonder if I should go up the mountain, or down it, or simply go round it. I suppose *down* is the obvious choice. I don't suppose for one moment Oddfellows' Hall is at the top of a mountain. Besides, the King did say he thought I was too high up, and down is certainly the easiest way to go."

So she set off, crunching through the snow (into which the cherry blossom petals had mysteriously turned). It was heavy going and Alice dearly wished she had some snowshoes. Before long, a building came into view, below her on the mountainside. As she approached, she was able to make out it was the station and winding-house at the top of a cable railway.

She ran as best she could over the last few yards and, kicking the snow from her shoes, went inside. Beside the turnstile sat a uniformed ticket inspector in a booth. The cable-car looked ready to depart. The door was closed and it was nearly full of passengers—most of them people dressed in skiing gear with woolly hats, but there were several cows also.

"Am I in time to catch the cable-car?" Alice asked the ticket inspector.

"I don't see how you could catch it, in time or not," replied the inspector gruffly. "It's much too heavy for one thing, and for another, we never drop it."

Alice rephrased her question. "I mean, am I in time to get on board? It looks as if there are a few places left in the car. I would rather like to get off this mountain, you see."

"I see," said the inspector with a sniff. "Have you got a ticket?"

"No, I'm sorry, I haven't. Can you sell me one?"

"I don't sell tickets here, miss. You have to get them from the bottom station."

"But how do I get to the bottom if I ca'n't ride in the cable-car?" protested Alice. "Besides, once I get to the bottom I sha'n't need a ticket any more."

"You should have thought of that and bought a return ticket before you came up," responded the inspector with very little sympathy, as he started to punch a few holes in his lapel with his ticket punch.

"I didn't come here by cable-car," explained Alice, getting more than a little frustrated. "In fact, I'm not at all sure how I *did* get here, but that's beside the point. Couldn't I just go to the bottom and pay when I get there?"

"Certainly not. That would never do. Sorry, no ticket, no seat."

"I wouldn't mind standing," said Alice meekly, but the inspector wasn't listening. He stood up and pulled a large lever, and the cable-car groaned slowly into motion and started upon its journey down the mountain.

"Really!" snorted Alice, thoroughly annoyed. "I think you might have been a *little* more helpful. I wonder you have any customers left if you treat them so. How on earth am I to get down now?"

"There'll be another car in half an hour," replied the ticket inspector, totally unconcerned.

"Can I board that one without a ticket?"

"'Course not, but with half an hour to spare, you could always pop down to the bottom and buy one."

The inspector took out an illustrated magazine and started to read, avoiding Alice's glare. Infuriated, she turned and stomped out of the station.

Oddly, the snow seemed to have vanished. There was grass underfoot, punctuated with little clumps of buttercups. A few yards away the Cow, still wearing skis, was staring at her and chewing the cud.

"I don't suppose you know how I can get to Oddfellows' Hall," asked Alice forlornly.

"Moo," replied the Cow sadly, and Alice had a suspicion that the Cow shook her head, but she couldn't be sure.

Just then, a shrill stern voice from behind made her jump. "There you are, young lady. We have been looking for you everywhere. Come along, the party is about to begin."

Turning round, Alice was almost glad to find herself face to face with the Red Queen. She was feeling so lost that any familiar face would have cheered her up—even one as miserable as the Queen's.

"You shouldn't wander off like that," continued the Queen. "I have had the whole of the royal household out looking for you. Why do I always find things in the last place I look?"

"Because once you've found them you stop looking, silly," said the Cow suddenly.

"You can talk!" said Alice accusingly. "Why didn't you answer me when I asked you the way?"

"Moo," replied the Cow.

"Come along," urged the Queen impatiently. "We ca'n't stand around chatting all day. We shall be late."

"How do we get to Oddfellows' Hall from here?" asked Alice. "I keep on asking people but none of them seem to be able to help me."

"That's because you ca'n't get to Oddfellows' Hall at all from here," replied the Queen. "To get to Oddfellows' Hall, you need to start off from somewhere else entirely."

"It must be possible somehow," protested Alice. "You ca'n't just not be able to get somewhere. Why don't we start by going to the 'somewhere else' from which we can get to Oddfellows' Hall and then carry on to Oddfellows' Hall from there?"

The Queen looked very puzzled and scratched her head. She stared up at the sky and then down at her feet. She stood completely silent, fixed in that pose, for several minutes, her forehead wrinkled in a deep frown. Alice was almost convinced she had turned back into a wooden chess piece but then she looked up and smiled.

"Chocolate cake!" shouted the Queen triumphantly, as if she had just solved some great problem. "Come on." She grabbed Alice's hand and set off across the grass.

"Steady," Alice called out. "You're hurting my arm. I do wish folk wouldn't rush so."

"You need to get your skates on if you want to get to the ball on time," replied the Queen, thrusting a pair of roller-skates into Alice's free hand.

"I'm afraid I ca'n't put these on with one hand while we're running along. We'll have to stop for a moment."

Mercifully, the Queen stopped. Alice sat down on the ground and put on the skates while the Queen stood beside her, scouring the horizon with one hand shading her eyes.

"There's no time to be lost, young lady," said the Queen sternly. "We must get a move on. It will be dark by nightfall."

The observation seemed self evident to Alice so she declined to comment. She finished lacing the roller-skates and rose, rather unsteadily, to her feet.

"Right, off we go," said the Queen, and gave Alice a firm push in the back. The skates must have been good ones because Alice immediately set off down the hillside. Rapidly she gathered speed, completely out of control and unable to stop herself.

"I do hope there's something soft at the bottom of this slope," thought Alice. Her hopes were in vain. "Oh dear. I do believe there's a brick wall across at the bottom. Why don't they make roller-skates with brakes?"

A collision seemed unavoidable. Alice hoped it wouldn't prove too painful. "At least I shall stop at last," she consoled herself.

When it came, the crash was painless. There was no cement holding together the large wooden blocks making up the wall and she piled into it, sending several of them flying.

"Oh!" exclaimed Alice in surprise. "Why, these building blocks have got white faces on the under-side with all sorts of strange designs on them. Circles and Chinese characters. If I didn't know any better, I should say they were tiles from a Mah-jong set."

CHAPTER X

The Mah-jong Dragons

"Clearly you don't know any better," said a voice, giving Alice something of a shock. Peering at her through the hole she had just made in the wall were three Dragons, one Red, one Green, and one White.

"I don't know any better than what?" asked Alice.

"You said if you didn't know any better you would say the blocks were Mah-jong pieces," continued the Green Dragon. "Well, they *are* Mah-jong pieces, so you don't know any better."

"What's going on?" asked the White Dragon. He seemed a bit older than the others and sounded more than a little irritated.

"It's a young girl. She's broken the wall," replied the Green Dragon.

"What's that you say? A pung of what?" asked the White Dragon, twisting his neck to bring his left ear closer to the conversation.

The Green Dragon raised his voice a little. "Not a *pung* of anything. A *young* girl. She's broken the wall."

98

"Oh," the White Dragon turned to Alice. "Are you East Wind then?"

"I'm not a wind at all."

"What's that she said?" asked the White Dragon, addressing the Green.

"She says she isn't a wind at all."

"Pardon?" said the White Dragon, and he produced a large brass ear-trumpet from beneath his right wing and held it to his ear.

The Green Dragon bellowed into the trumpet. "SHE SAYS SHE ISN'T A WIND AT ALL."

"Not a wind? Not a wind?" repeated the White Dragon angrily. "What's she doing breaking the wall? Only East Wind can break the wall."

Alice apologized. "I didn't mean to break the wall. It was an accident. Was it very valuable?"

"Invaluable," sighed the Green Dragon sadly. "It's taken hours to build. Now we shall have to do it all over again before we can play the next hand." He sighed again, and two thin curls of grey smoke drifted up from his nostrils.

"Would this be a suitable moment to ask

whether you know the way to Oddfellows' Hall?" asked Alice, anxious to change the subject.

"I suppose it would," said the Green Dragon, a little reluctantly. "Are you, in fact, going to ask?"

"I thought I just had."

"Not at all," the Green Dragon said. "You merely asked if it were a suitable moment for the question."

"If you could just be a little less pedantic, I'm sure we should get on a lot better," said Alice, rather pompously. "Is it far to Oddfellows' Hall? Do you know the way?"

"Not far at all, really," replied the Green Dragon. "We could get there in a trice, except we haven't got a trice."

It was then that the Red Dragon broke his silence. "We could always fly her there," he suggested. He spoke with a soft Welsh accent and it came as an immense relief to Alice to find someone being helpful for a change.

"You mean you can actually fly?" asked Alice.

"Of course," said the Red Dragon. "Don't tell me you've never seen a dragon fly."

"No," admitted Alice.

"You should go down to your local pond," suggested the Green Dragon. "You see dragonflies there all the time."

"I don't think that's what your friend meant," replied Alice. "I meant I have never seen a dragon flying."

"Of course not," scoffed the Green Dragon, with a haughty laugh. "There's no such creature as a dragonflying."

"What's going on?" asked the White Dragon. "What are you mumbling about?"

"Red Dragon suggests we should fly this young lady to Oddfellows' Hall!" shouted the Green Dragon, so loudly it made Alice's ears hurt.

"No that would never do," objected the White Dragon. "We shouldn't fry her. Little girls are much better stewed."

Alice was more than a little alarmed by this last remark, but the Red Dragon reassured her. "Pay no attention to him. He doesn't really eat young girls, but his mind does tend to wander a bit."

"Sometimes I think it has wandered off entirely," added the Green Dragon. "However, I agree with my colleague. We may as well fly you there. We ca'n't carry on with the game with the wall in ruins, and I ca'n't be bothered to build it up again. You may as well hop on."

Alice clambered up onto the Green Dragon's back. The bright green feathers were remarkably soft and comfortable—just like an enormous feather bed. Once she had settled down, the Green and Red Dragons unfolded their wings and, with slow powerful flaps, they set off into the air. The White Dragon, who had not heard the preceding conversation and only realized what was happening when he saw his companions set off, followed on behind.

"Splendid place for a party, Oddfellows' Hall," commented the Green Dragon to his passenger. "I'm rather looking forward to it."

"Yes," agreed the Red Dragon. "Our local wine circle meets there every week."

"What's that?" puffed the White Dragon who had just managed to catch up with them. "Did somebody say 'nine circles'? Chow."

The other two ignored him. The Red Dragon reached under his feathers, pulled out a large cigar and lit it. He did all this without the slightest interruption to the rhythm of his beating wings—no mean achievement, Alice thought. He puffed on the cigar a couple of times and then, much to Alice's surprise, ate it while still alight, chewing thoughtfully and with apparent relish.

"Doesn't it burn your throat, eating cigars?" enquired Alice.

"Good heavens no," retorted the Red Dragon. "Fire is a dragon's staple diet, along with curry, mustard, and horseradish sauce. Would you like one?"

"No, thank you," said Alice. "Will the journey take long?"

"Hush!" hissed the Green Dragon suddenly, turning his head round so far that it faced in completely the wrong direction, looking backwards towards her. The request for silence was delivered with such urgency that a few sparks spilled from his mouth along with the "sh", singeing the feathers in front of Alice. "There is an oyse coming."

Alice peered ahead, trying to work out what the Green Dragon was talking about. She would dearly have loved to ask exactly what an oyse was (the word was pronounced to rhyme with *boys*), but feared to do so after the Green Dragon's urgent request for silence.

Holding her hand to her forehead to shield her eyes from the sun, she could just make out what looked like a large bird in the distance.

For several seconds, the little formation of

Dragons flew on in silence. The bird, which Alice soon discovered was flying towards them, got nearer and nearer.

After a short while, she was able to make it out more clearly. She had never seen a bird with feathers of so many different colours. Those on the wing were bright crimson tipped with yellow, while its tail was emerald green. Its head was purple with an orange crest, while the down on its chest was deep royal blue. Its wingspan must have been all of twelve feet, yet it swam through the sky almost effortlessly and in total silence. Even the enormous wings made not the slightest sound as it swept majestically through the air.

Alice had the distinct impression the bird smiled at her as it passed, although how something so thoroughly unpliable as a beak could form itself into a smile, she could not imagine. She watched over her shoulder as the bird slowly disappeared into the distance.

When it was visible no more, she turned back. The Green Dragon's head was still looking backwards and Alice wondered how he dared to fly without looking where he was going.

"What was that?" she asked.

"An oyse of course," replied the Green Dragon, slightly contemptuously. "Surely you know what an oyse looks like."

"No," said Alice. "I'm afraid they don't have them where I come from. Why did we have to be so quiet?"

"It's all those bright feathers," explained the Red Dragon. "The oyse always has a terrible headache, having to look at those bright colours on its friends and on itself."

The Green Dragon began to recite:

> *"A wondrous creature is the oyse.*
> *Silence, that's what it enjoys.*
> *So if by chance you find one out,*
> *Please don't laugh or scream or shout*
> *Or bang a drum or smash your toys,*
> *For such a noise annoys an oyse."*

"Perhaps they would be better off if they wore sunglasses," suggested Alice.

"I'm sure they would," agreed the Red Dragon. "However, I wouldn't suggest trying to tell the oyse that. They get awfully annoyed if you try to talk to them."

"It must be a terribly lonely life if no one dares talk to you," Alice commented.

"Oh they talk to each other, all right," said the Red Dragon. "But not using sounds. They signal to each other by waving their tail feathers. It is all very well, I suppose, but if you don't happen to have tail feathers you ca'n't join in the conversation."

Even so, Alice felt rather sorry for the creature with its lonely silent existence. She could not for one moment believe it possible to hold anything approaching an interesting conversation just by waving one's tail feathers. But her ponderings on the trials and tribulations of life for an oyse were brought to a halt by a strange metallic tinging noise, as if someone were striking a tiny bell.

The tinging noise proved to be the chime of a small pocket watch, which the Green Dragon pulled out from under his feathers.

"Good heavens, look how late it is. Time really has been enjoying himself." So saying, he swooped down and landed gently on the ground in a little clearing amongst some trees. His landing was closely followed by the Red Dragon. The White Dragon, who apparently failed to notice the others land, flew on.

"What do you mean, 'time has been enjoying himself'?" asked Alice as she clambered down from the Dragon's back.

"Exactly what I say," responded the Green Dragon. "If Time flies when you are enjoying yourself, it seems only fair Time should enjoy himself when you are flying."

"Quite so," agreed the Red Dragon. "Now it's breakfast time."

The Red Dragon pulled a large metal tray from under his wing. Alice wondered how on earth they had managed to fly with so many things tucked under their wings and feathers. The tray had collapsible legs and the Dragon unfolded them to form a little table.

"Are you absolutely sure it's breakfast time?" asked Alice a little dubiously. "I thought one normally ate breakfast first thing in the morning. I have been up for ages. It seems more like lunch time to me, possibly even tea time."

"Dragons only ever eat one meal a day," explained the Red Dragon. "So it's always the first meal of the day, and therefore breakfast."

"Of course, we generally eat at about midday," added the Green Dragon. "So it is lunch as well."

"In fact just after midday as a rule," continued the Red Dragon. "So I suppose you could call it afternoon tea. It's our main meal too, so we often call it dinner."

"And it's the last meal of the day," pointed out the Green Dragon, "so some would call it supper. Would you care for a slice of toast? Or perhaps you would prefer some bacon and eggs."

"Toast will do fine," Alice assured him.

"I'm sorry," the Green Dragon continued. "We don't have any bread, so you ca'n't have toast."

"Then why did you offer it?" asked Alice, curtly.

"I was merely trying to give you a choice," the Green Dragon defended. "Had you chosen bacon and eggs, you could have had your first choice. Besides, you might not actually like bacon and eggs, so it would be quite uncivil to insist you ate them."

Alice was far from convinced by the Green Dragon's arguments but decided further discussion was unlikely to be helpful. She therefore agreed that bacon and eggs would be a perfectly acceptable breakfast.

"Unfortunately, we have no eggs either," admitted the Green Dragon.

"Do you have any bacon?" asked Alice, who was beginning to wonder if there was, in fact, any food on offer at all.

"Of course, of course," replied the Green Dragon. "We have some lovely gammon rashers."

"Then I shall have some of that," agreed Alice.

During the latter part of the conversation, the Red Dragon had gathered some brushwood together and a couple of broken tree branches. He now took a deep breath and, turning to his bonfire, exhaled hard. Two great jets of flame leapt from his nostrils and within seconds, the fire was crackling and burning merrily.

The Green Dragon produced a large frying pan from beneath his tail feathers (it must have been all of three feet across) and placed it on the flames. Meanwhile the Red Dragon had produced a large flat box from which he started to remove some counters and toss them into the pan. This struck Alice as more than a little odd.

"Come now," said the Green Dragon. "We have visitors to-day. I think we may as well use the lot."

The Red Dragon opened the box out flat, and threw that in the pan also. The box had a regular pattern of triangles on it, two rows of six on each half.

"That's not gammon," protested Alice. "It's a backgammon set."

"That's right. The butcher said it was the best back gammon," the Green Dragon assured her.

"It's not back gammon, it's backgammon," repeated Alice. "One word, not two—it's a board game."

"Whether it's bored or interested in something, I don't see how gammon can be game," said the Red Dragon. "Only things like pheasant and venison are game."

"It does seem a bit tough," lamented the Green Dragon. "If it is game, perhaps we ought to hang it before we try to cook it."

"I'm not so sure it's proper back gammon at all you know," commented the Red Dragon. I'm still not convinced that 'butcher' is spelt T–O–Y–S–H–O–P."

It was at this moment that the White Dragon arrived. Being quite deaf, he had heard neither the alarm clock nor the discussions about breakfast. He came swooping down over the treetops, shouting at the top of his voice "Where is everyone? I wish folk would tell me when they are going to land. I thought we were going to Oddfellows' Hall. Where are you all?"

"He must be a little short -sighted as well as deaf," thought Alice. "I suppose one might be forgiven for missing the Green Dragon amongst the foliage, the Red one sticks out like a sore thumb."

Nevertheless, the White Dragon failed to see either of them and, despite Alice's urgent cries of "Watch out!', he skimmed along just above ground level and piled straight into the Green Dragon. The two rolled along together and collided with the Red Dragon, who in turn lost his footing and crashed into the fire. There were sparks flying everywhere. Some were from the fire, but several flew from the Dragons' mouths and nostrils as they rolled, grunting and wheezing, along the ground.

It only took a few seconds for some of the nearby bushes to catch light. The flames spread briskly, and Alice feared she might be caught in a forest fire.

She turned and ducked quickly through the trees, hoping the Dragons would be sensible enough to escape too.

CHAPTER XI

Rules and Races

*I*t did not take long for Alice to reach the edge of the trees. The last few trunks had notices pinned to them. Deciding she had put enough distance between herself and the fire to be out of danger, Alice paused long enough to read them.

THIS AFTERNOON: ANNUAL SUMMER SPORTS

read the first. The second added:

PRIZES FOR ALL.

Alice wondered whether that meant prizes for all entrants or prizes for all events. The last notice was completely out of character with the other two. Indeed Alice thought it rather rude. It read:

PLEASE DO NOT READ THIS NOTICE.

This
Afternoon:

Annual
Summer
Sports

Prizes
for
All

Please
Do Not
Read
This
Notice

Had
it not been
that such a
thing was clearly
impossible, Alice could
have sworn this last
notice stuck its tongue
out at her as she walked
past.

As she emerged from the wood,
Alice was slightly surprised to be greeted
by loud applause. A large congregation of creatures was
gathered on the grass in the shade of the trees. They were
mostly rats, mice, and other small rodents. Nearer the wood
(and well away from all the mice), a tabby cat was providing
background music, playing on a fiddle.

Standing out from the crowd were a fine Pheasant and a Peacock, who appeared to be in charge of proceedings, since they were strutting up and down shouting orders to everyone. The Pheasant had a whistle round his neck, and this he blew every few seconds, to reinforce his authority.

When the applause subsided, he marched over to Alice, blew the whistle louder than ever right next to her ear, then said "Congratulations. You're the winner."

"Winner of what?" asked Alice, a little confused.

"Why, the balloon race, of course," said the Pheasant. "You've come in first."

"But I didn't even know I was in the race," protested Alice.

"All the cleverer to have won it then," said the Peacock, who had strolled over to join them.

"I haven't even got a balloon," continued Alice. "Don't I need one for a balloon race?"

"No balloon?" said the Pheasant, slightly perplexed. "We shall have to see what the rules say about that."

He took a small book from his waistcoat pocket ("Strange," thought Alice, "that I never noticed his bright red waistcoat before. It's brighter than the Peacock's tail!") The Pheasant leafed through the book in an agitated fashion, blowing his whistle intermittently.

"Enough of rules," said the Peacock, snatching the book from his companion and throwing it to the ground. "If we disqualify her, we shall be here all day waiting for the winner because there's no one else in the race. Just give her a balloon and get on with the next race."

He produced a yellow balloon from his own waistcoat pocket (which again, Alice had previously failed to notice), and stuck it on the end of the Pheasant's whistle. The Pheasant blew the whistle a few more times to inflate the balloon then the Peacock removed it and handed it to Alice.

This seemed to be the signal for a great deal more applause, and the Pheasant took out a large toy drum from his waistcoat pocket. He banged on it three times, at which the crowd hushed again. The drum was actually larger than the waistcoat, and Alice could not help but wonder how he had managed to conceal it.

"Three cheers for the balloon race winner," shouted the Peacock. The crowd cheered three times. "Now," he said, turning to Alice, "if you would be so kind as to rejoin the others, it is time for the custard race."

Alice walked over in the direction indicated by the Peacock. A small band of mice and voles were already limbering up, most of them wearing running shorts.

"Excuse me," said Alice to a small grey Mouse in red shorts. "What precisely *is* a custard race?"

Before the Mouse had time to reply, the Pheasant interrupted. 'On your marks, get set, GO!"

At this command, the little creatures began to scurry about in all directions. None of them looked as if they knew what to do, or which way to run. One of them collided with the Pheasant, who blew angrily on his whistle. The Peacock was banging out a slow rhythm on his drum, each bang sounding almost exactly like the noise of a dripping tap. One of the voles then tripped up the Peacock, who dropped his drum and then trod on it. His foot went straight through and thick yellow custard began to emerge from the crack.

The Pheasant, who had now recovered his footing, marched over to Alice and blurted out "There's no cause for alarm."

"I'm not at all alarmed," Alice assured him. "Why should I be?"

"No reason at all," said the Pheasant. "I merely wanted to assure you that if you were considering becoming alarmed, you have no cause."

By this time the custard, which was still gushing from the hole in the drum, had spread out over almost the entire area. It was getting deeper by the moment and soon came over the top of Alice's shoes.

"Quickly," urged a brown Mouse at Alice's side, "Find a spoon. We must eat this custard before we all drown."

The custard had already reached up to Alice's chest. The next minute it swept her off her feet and she found herself

carried away on a vast, fast-running yellow river. The Pheasant swept past, still blowing his whistle and flapping his wings, making terrible splashes. "Stop this!" he shouted, before blowing his whistle again. "This isn't in the rules!" And so he continued, alternately shouting and blowing his whistle, until he was (thankfully) out of earshot.

Although Alice would scarcely admit it, even to herself, at that moment she would have been glad to see the Dog and his rowing boat. Instead, she thought she could just make out something vaguely boat-like, a few yards away, into which a number of mice and other creatures were clambering.

She swam in that direction and a few moments later was helped on board the little craft by a slightly damp Vole.

"You know," remarked Alice to her rescuer, "this looks more like the bowl of a spoon than a boat."

"How right you are," replied the Vole. "This is the last leg of the custard race."

"Don't be ridiculous," snapped a white Mouse, seated beside the Vole. "Custard races don't have legs."

At this point, the little craft (or spoon as it turned out to be) lifted gracefully into the air, and a few seconds later deposited its occupants onto the grass.

"Congratulations." Alice looked up. It was the Peacock who was speaking. "You've won the custard race as well. We shall have to find you a prize."

"Yes indeed," added the Pheasant. He appeared to have recovered his composure, although his waistcoat had turned yellow. "Such achievements call for a prize."

"Excuse me." This time it was a pale brown Hamster speaking. "I wish to raise an objection. The young lady cheated."

"I did not," said Alice indignantly. Although she didn't actually know the rules, she felt sure she had done nothing which could be considered cheating.

"Stuff and nonsense!" said the Pheasant, and he produced a bright silver cup from his apparently bottomless waistcoat pocket and held it out to Alice—but the Hamster grabbed it and stuffed it into his mouth. A moment later, the cup was nothing but a bulge in the Hamster's cheek.

"Arrest that Hamster," shouted the Pheasant. "He's eaten the prize."

"Don't worry," said the Peacock quietly. "I shall paint her a picture as a prize. Let's get on with the egg and spoon race."

This last suggestion came as a relief to Alice. At last there was to be a race she understood. She always did fairly well in the egg and spoon race on the annual sports day at her school.

"Where do I go for the egg and spoon race?" she asked.

The Pheasant frowned at her. "Which are you—egg or spoon?" he asked suspiciously.

"I'm not either," said Alice, puzzled. "I thought one merely had to carry an egg on a spoon."

"Stuff and nonsense!" said the Pheasant. "Only eggs and spoons are allowed in egg and spoon races. If we allowed little girls, it would be called a girl, egg, and spoon race."

He strode over to where a number of eggs—each of which had legs and was wearing running clothes—were lining up. Alice followed in order to get a better view of the proceedings.

"Where is the Spoon?" asked the Pheasant gruffly. "I'm sure there was at least one in the original entry."

The nearest Egg piped up in a high squeaky voice "I'm sorry sir, but the Dish ran away with him. It's only us left."

"Well, that is no good at all," said the Pheasant crossly. "You ca'n't have an egg and spoon race without any spoon." He turned to Alice. "I don't suppose you would consider turning into a spoon?"

Alice had to admit she had no idea how to achieve such a thing, even if she wanted to. The Pheasant looked at her suspiciously, as if he did not fully believe her.

"Well, that's it," he said. "We shall have to cancel the race."

He wandered back to the Peacock. The Peacock had set up an easel and was standing with his back to it painting a picture of the event with his tail feathers. It looked to Alice as though he was a real expert with the brush. Her only criticism was he was painting the entire scene upside down.

"What now?" asked the Pheasant. "The egg and spoon race has had to be cancelled—the Dish has run away with the Spoon."

The Peacock consulted a piece of paper from his waistcoat pocket. "Cows' high jump is the next event," he announced.

The program of events had a familiar ring to Alice, although at the time she could not think why. Somehow she must have missed the cows' high jump event because the next thing she knew, the winners were being announced.

"Congratulations," said the Pheasant. He was addressing the Cow, which Alice thought must be the same one she had encountered on the mountain earlier, since she was still wearing her skis. "Here is your prize." The Pheasant handed the Cow a large Swiss cheese, full of holes.

"Moo," said the Cow.

"What did she say?" asked the Pheasant of the Peacock. "Is she happy with her prize?"

"She said she's over the moon about it," replied the Peacock.

"Splendid," said the Pheasant. "What is the next event?"

"Snakes and ladders," replied his colleague.

"Oh, even more splendid. My favourite event. Come on, every one. Time for snakes and ladders."

Now, Alice had played snakes and ladders many times, and had never considered it an outdoor sport—but the assembled crowd were clearly in the habit of playing it that way. The Pheasant's announcement was the signal for a great deal of excitement and frenzied activity.

A small group of white rats made themselves busy laying ropes across the ground, first in one direction then the other. There seemed to be several accidents along the way when one or more of the other creatures got tangled up in the ropes, but they eventually managed to divide the area into neat squares. The squares extended as far as Alice could see, in every direction.

Meanwhile, a number of hamsters and field mice had obtained an enormous selection of ladders in various sizes (Alice never did discover where they all came from), and laid them across the squares or, in some cases, propped them up against trees. One mouse even propped a ladder against the Peacock, at which the Peacock was decidedly unamused.

By the time all this frenzied activity had finished, the whole scene looked like an enormous snakes-and-ladders board. The only things missing (to Alice's immense relief) were snakes.

CHAPTER XII

Snakes and Ladders

$\mathcal{A}$ lice quickly found out why, in present company, snakes and ladders was considered an outdoor sport. "No one seems to be taking turns," she thought. "Mind you, it is probably just as well. With such a large number of players, one might have to wait several weeks for one's turn to come round."

Instead, the players rolled the dice at every opportunity. There were many dice in use, but not enough for each player to have one, so fights often broke out as contestants tried to get hold of one. Many of those left without dice were undeterred and moved anyway. Alice wondered if there were any rules at all, and if so, if anyone was making sure the players kept to them.

To add to the general confusion, the dice were considerably larger than the most of the players. Some contestants took advantage of this and deliberately rolled the dice at their opponents in an attempt to knock them over. Often they succeeded and before long there were as many players sprawling on the ground as there were moving about.

Once she got into it, Alice rather enjoyed the game, although it was a little frustrating having to fight for the dice (Alice was far too honest to move without throwing). Nearly every time she moved she ended up at the foot of a ladder and had to hobble along it to another square.

"I have noticed a very curious thing about ladders," she remarked to a nearby Dormouse, who was pinned to the ground under a particularly large die. "They are so much harder to climb when they are lying on the ground. Can I help you at all?"

"I should be most grateful if you could move this die," replied the Dormouse. "It is rather heavy."

Alice pushed the die aside. The Dormouse stood up and gave her a gracious bow. "That's extremely kind of you miss. I am most honoured to make your acquaintance. Would you care to toss the die for both of us?"

Alice could see why the Dormouse didn't want to throw for himself. The die was almost too heavy for her to lift and the Dormouse was a fraction of her size. She just managed to heave it so it rolled over a couple of times before coming to rest with a six uppermost.

"Well done," cheered the Dormouse, clapping his hands together excitedly. "May I have the pleasure of escorting you the next six squares?"

He held out his arm, which Alice took, and together they strolled forward. The six squares seemed to take them away from the main throng and towards the edge of the wood. In the sixth square they found a tall oak tree with a ladder propped against it. The top of the ladder was lost in the branches.

"After you, Miss," said the Dormouse, releasing Alice's arm and pointing towards the ladder.

"It seems to me," said Alice, "that if we climb this ladder, we shall be out of the game. There ca'n't be any further squares up in the branches of a tree, can there?"

"I don't suppose so," agreed the Dormouse. "But you never know, we could find the top of the tree is 'home', and we've won."

"The top of an oak tree seems like a very odd place to choose as 'home'," said Alice, a little dubiously. "Mind you, I've seen plenty of things a lot odder in the last little while, and I suppose the ladder has to be here for some purpose."

With slight misgivings, Alice started to climb. As she did so, the Dormouse said something else to her, which she didn't quite catch, although afterwards she decided it might have been something in the nature of "Or it might just lead to a snake."

That certainly wasn't how she heard it at the time, or she would have been much more nervous as she climbed the ladder.

"Oh!" exclaimed Alice somewhat disappointedly, when she finally reached the top. "There is nothing here except branches and leaves. How is one supposed to carry on playing from here?"

She called down to the Dormouse. "It doesn't look like the finish. Are you coming up, or do you think I should come down again?" But there was no reply.

There was one advantage to being up the tree. From her high vantage point Alice had a perfect view of the rest of the game. It looked even more disorganized (if such a thing were possible) than it had when she had been down amongst the players. She was just settling down to her grandstand view when she first heard the noise. It was so quiet at first that one might have been excused for missing it altogether. Alice wasn't sure whether to describe it as a rustling noise or as a hissing noise. In either case, it didn't sound a very safe sort of noise to leave uninvestigated. For some reason, Alice found it most disconcerting.

"It seems to be coming from the next branch but one," she thought and, feeling very brave, she clambered gingerly from her branch to the next, hoping to find the cause of the perplexing little rustle—or was it a hiss? From the next branch, the noise seemed to be exactly as far away as it had before, so she climbed onto the next one, then the next, then the next. Several times she tried to move towards the noise but each time it made no difference. She could not get any nearer. Eventually she gave up and sat down again.

"This really is a most frustrating tree," Alice declared. "It seems to be growing as I sit in it. Every time I climb onto a branch, another one seems to spring up between me and the one I'm trying to get to. No matter how many branches I clamber over, the noise always seems to be coming from the next but one."

The rustling noise continued. "This is really most inconsiderate of you!" she shouted at the noise. "I've never come across a sound that runs away before—but I've had *enough*, I tell you! You can run away as much as you please. I'm just going to watch the snakes and ladders."

She turned her back on the noise rather sulkily. Then a rather worrying notion came into her mind. The noise did sound just a little like a snake. Not that Alice had ever met any snakes, but it sounded just as she imagined a snake might sound were she to chance upon one.

"Perhaps it's just as well it always stays a couple of branches away," she thought. "In fact, I think I've had quite enough of sitting in this tree. If only I could find my way back to the ladder..."

Alice started to retrace her steps, trying to work her way back to the branch she had started from but as soon as she did, something rather worrying happened. As she retreated across the branches, the hissing noise followed her.

"Considering things logically," she thought to herself, "I am no worse off. The noise is always on the next branch but one, whether I move towards it or away from it. Why then does it seem so much more uncomfortable to have a noise follow me rather than the other way round?"

It was at that moment Alice noticed the noise was no longer on the next branch but one. It was on the very next branch— or was it even her own branch?

"Oh!" gasped Alice, suddenly finding herself face to face with the largest snake she had ever seen. (This seems less remarkable when you consider it was also the first snake she had ever seen in the flesh.)

Had she the time and composure to consider the matter, Alice would have been more than a little puzzled by the manner of the snake's arrival. She had not turned to discover that it had crept up on her. There was no turning involved. It was simply that one moment it wasn't there and the next it was. At the time, though, Alice was far too concerned about its mere presence to wonder how it had come to be there.

"Good afternoon," she said, as politely as she could. Alice was not sure of the correct way to address a snake but was particularly eager not to anger it. "Splendid afternoon for a game, isn't it?"

"Indeed sso," hissed the snake, and it licked its lips several times with its forked tongue.

"What... kind of snake are you?" asked Alice, looking at the pattern of reddish brown markings on the snake's back. "Are you poisonous?"

"I am a Boa," it said. "We are not poisonouss. We ssqueeze the prey we eat."

"I hope you don't intend to eat me," added Alice, immediately regretting she might have put such an idea into the creature's mind.

"Why not?" asked the Boa.

"Well, for one thing," Alice replied, "I don't suppose I should taste very nice, and for another, I don't think it's very polite to eat people the first time you meet them. We haven't even been formally introduced."

"I don't ssee how that matters," said the Boa, licking its lips again. "Far better, surely, to eat ssomeone you don't know very well than a closse friend. The mosst important rule is not to eat people the lasst time you meet them."

"That must be a very difficult rule to keep," said Alice, puzzled. "How can you be sure you are going to see someone again, so you can safely eat them? I should have thought you were most unlikely to see someone again after you have eaten them."

"Not in thiss game," said the Boa. "When I eat people, they end up further back down the board sso they always have to come passt me again."

Alice was slightly reassured by the Boa's suggestion that she would still be able to walk about and greet people despite having been eaten, but she was not entirely convinced she believed it. She decided the safest course was to talk about something else for a bit to see if she could make the snake forget the whole idea.

"I didn't know snakes could climb trees. Isn't it rather hard without any legs?"

"Not at all," replied the Boa. "Indeed, I should have thought those ssilly leg things would get in the way. If I were you, I should try doing without them. Would you like me to eat them for you?"

"Certainly not," said Alice, alarmed. It seemed to be almost impossible to steer the snake away from the subject of eating.

She tried to find a safe topic of conversation. "It's a very pleasant day for a game isn't it?"

"I ssuppose it'ss all very well if you like that ssort of thing, but I'm afraid all thiss running about jusst makess me hungry. Anyway, it'ss time for the next sstage of the game now. Do you think you could give me a hand?"

"What with?" asked Alice, eager to help, and hoping any diversion would cause the snake to stop going on about hunger and food. "What is the next stage of the game?"

"Why, eating you of coursse," replied the Boa. "And I don't want the hand with anything. I jusst thought I might eat it on itss own, for sstarters."

"I should far rather you didn't," pleaded Alice.

"Tell you what," suggested the Boa, "jusst to make it fair, we'll sstart off doing it your way, and I wo'n't eat you. Then we'll take a turn doing it my way, and I shall."

"I don't see how that's fair," protested Alice. "I don't want you to eat me at all."

"We musst follow the rules," insisted the Boa. "If you're not going to co-operate, I shall jusst have to eat you whole and have done with it."

Then the Boa opened its mouth wide and, without giving her time for further objection, swallowed Alice in one enormous gulp.

CHAPTER **XIII**

From Boa to Bedroom

*I*t was very dark inside the snake. For a while, Alice felt
herself being swept along, until at last she came to a
halt. It was like being in a small dark tunnel except the walls
were spongy.

She pushed her way along a bit further, pushing out the
walls whenever the tunnel was too small to squeeze through.
After a while, she thought she could see something light
ahead. With renewed energy, she forged her way forward only
to find that the tunnel came, rather abruptly, to an end. In a
last fit of desperation, Alice pushed hard against the soft walls
at the end of the tunnel. To her surprise, they parted and, to
her even greater surprise, she found what she had done was to
untuck her covers and emerge at the foot of her bed.

Fortunately, the bed no longer looked anything like a boat
and was standing securely (and completely stationary) on the
floor of her bedroom.

"Oh," said Alice. After overcoming her initial surprise, she
was slightly disappointed. "I suppose, in some ways, it is a

relief not to have been digested, but I was rather enjoying the game."

It occurred to her that if she made her way back under the bed covers she might be able to emerge through the snake's mouth, find herself back in the tree, and then be able to climb down to rejoin the game. But when she tried it, she just ended up back at her pillow.

Dinah, who had been knocked off the bed with all this tunnelling back and forth, was sitting on the floor looking up at Alice reproachfully. She managed a plaintive "mew" as Alice's head emerged from the covers once more.

"It's a great pity you weren't with me, Dinah darling," said Alice gently. "You would have had such fun chasing the mice across the snakes-and-ladders board."

She got up and remade her bed. Then, picking up Dinah, she climbed back into bed and set the kitten down next to her on the pillow.

"I've all sorts of adventures to tell you," said Alice. "If only you hadn't run away when that dog came, you could have come too."

The kitten gave Alice a lick on the nose.

Alice started to explain how she had come to be on the boat and what had happened next, but she didn't get very far at all before her eyelids felt very heavy indeed. A moment later, she shut them and was fast asleep.

Lightning Source UK Ltd.
Milton Keynes UK
09 October 2009

144721UK00001B/17/P